Manhattan
Road Trip

Short Stories

Robin Meloy Goldsby

Copyright ©2016 Robin Meloy Goldsby
All rights reserved

ISBN-13: 9781523374229
ISBN-10: 1523374225

Library of Congress Control Number: 2016901022
CreateSpace Independent Publishing Platform
North Charleston, South Carolina

This is a Bass Lion book, published in the United States.
www.basslionpublishing.com

Front cover image of Karolina Strassmayer by photographer Helge Strauss
www.helge-strauss.de

Author photo of Robin Meloy Goldsby by Andreas Biesenbach
www.abproevent.de

Manufactured in the United States of America

Table of Contents

Rouge Noir	1
The Girl with the Flaxen Hair	15
Song for Alice	27
Hungry	35
Manhattan Road Trip	45
Sisterhood of Soul	55
Black Keys	65
Carol of the Bells	67
Pink	81
The Grand Handini	89
No Nonsense Fairy	97
Silver	103
Taps	109
Acknowledgements	117
About the Author	121
Also by Robin Meloy Goldsby	123

"Tones sound, and roar and storm about me until I have set them down in notes." Ludwig van Beethoven

⧝

"You are the music while the music lasts." T. S. Eliot

⧝

"You've got to get a job first. Then you've got to get *to* the job. And then, when that job is over, you have to get another job. Anyone teach you *that* in music school?" Your Uncle Manny

To working musicians everywhere—you are my heroes.

Rouge Noir

Alarm rings. B-flat. Fingers tingle; they always tingle on concert days. Wish I could start my morning with meditation. Been awake for an hour, worrying, fretting, betting something horrible will happen in the next twelve hours. Twelve hours. Got to get through half a day before I walk onstage this evening. So much easier if I could hop out of bed, into the shower, and onto the piano bench. Performance isn't hard—waiting kills me. Playing the Rachmaninoff Concerto No. 3 in D minor this evening with the Pittsburgh Symphony. Performed the Rach 3 at least thirty times over the last decade. Still kicks my butt. Like running a marathon in thirty-five minutes.

Sheets tangle between my legs, my hair tangles between my fingers, my stomach tangles in knots. Slightly nauseated. Hope I'm not pregnant again. Hope I don't have stomach cancer. Hope I didn't eat bad shrimp last night at Fred's Fish Factory. Why did I let that chirpy concert promoter talk me into eating crustaceans in a landlocked town? What's her name? Right. Madison. I'm an idiot when I'm hungry. I'll eat anything. Hope the zipper closes on my gown tonight. Should fast today—no, last time I tried that I fainted two hours before my New York Phil concert. Ended up drinking a vanilla milkshake to revive. Stomach bloated from the lactose. Rachmaninoff and bloat. Bad combo.

I hope the hair guy shows up. I hate big concert halls with balconies. People sitting above see my roots; high-rent folks in orchestra seats see my double chin. I'm screwed in two ticket-price tiers.

Wish they would just close their eyes and listen.

I really need to play the damn piano; always makes me feel better to play, at least in real life. Crawled into bed last night out of sorts and full of doom. Finally conked out, had a nightmare someone splattered the Steinway keyboard with olive oil. I've had this nightmare on the eve of every concert performance for fifteen years. Always the same—fingers slip and slide, and my performance, no matter what I do, veers from controlled elegance to sadistic slapstick. The audience laughs. I stand to leave the stage, humiliated and broken. I notice oil stains on my red evening gown. Guy in the front row of my dream looks exactly like Mr. Dominick, my childhood piano teacher. He wears a houndstooth jacket with mustard-colored suede elbow patches. "See?" he snarls. "I told you. You're no good. And not only that, you're fat." Then I wake up.

Enough.

I am Samantha Lockney. Used to be the toast of the classical piano world, girl with the platinum fingers, sweetheart of music critics everywhere, except in parts of Ohio, where, for some odd reason, they've always hated my emotional interpretations of Baroque music. They also hated me in Duluth and Phoenix. Fine with that. I am. Don't know anyone in Ohio, or Duluth, or Phoenix, except for my agent's mother. Met her once, when I played the A minor Brahms with the Cleveland Orchestra. My hands aren't really big enough for Brahms, so I had to stretch like crazy. That was back when I had big banging balls and I still tried to play pieces that didn't suit me. Before the agency and Classical

International Records started promoting me as a glamour girl. Back when I didn't have to worry about sucking in my stomach and wearing false eyelashes. Now, when I should be exhaling and leaning into the best years of my career, I face dwindling audiences, dismal record sales, and a substantial slab of flab around my middle. Not so noticeable when I'm upright, but I can't perform the Rachmaninoff Piano Concerto No. 3 in D minor if I'm not sitting down.

I hate sounding like a whining, weight-obsessed, middle-aged woman, but . . . If I'm not at the piano, I'm standing in front of a mirror freaking about how I *look* at the piano. Twenty years ago, on my agent's advice, I poured myself into a silver slip dress and jiggled onstage at Carnegie Hall. I actually believed, silver dress and all, the audience understood and admired my music. Wasn't the music they dug, it was the *package*. That's what the record company called me—a package. Yeah, I was talented. Yeah, I mastered Rach 3 when very few women even considered playing it. Yeah, I was the new kid on the scene. But I really got noticed for being classical piano's "It Girl." Or was it "Tit Girl"? Now the "It" part is gone; tits are sagging; career is tanking. I'm scared. I need to keep working. I need guidance. My own stupid fault. Other concert pianists have survived middle age without losing momentum—but they built careers on solid music, not on how they looked in a silver dress.

Classical International didn't pick up the option for my next recording, so now I'm a free agent. Therapist says anger gets me nowhere. Agent says anger gets me nowhere. Accountant says anger gets me nowhere. I pay a staff of professionals thousands of dollars a month to piss me off and tell me I'm getting nowhere. This morning, nowhere features a junior suite with two red velveteen chairs, king-sized bed, pink marble bathroom, and too many mirrors. The suite is a little smaller than my usual offerings—okay, a lot smaller—but the birdish Madison, a zipper-thin twenty-something, told me the pop singer Baby checked in yesterday and her handlers insisted on the Governor's Suite, the one originally reserved for me. I'm at the William Penn Hotel in downtown Pittsburgh. Didn't make a scene about the suite. I was tempted. It feels, I don't know, a little insulting to be jostled out of position by a chlorine-blond named Baby. We're both from Pittsburgh. Read somewhere she went to my elementary school, twenty years after I was there.

Saw pictures of Baby in *Vanity Fair* last month. She was wearing a latex mermaid costume. Even with flippers and fishtail, she's a looker. I remember how that used to feel. Seas parted, doors opened, men with coffee breath and thinning hair stared at my breasts and told me I was *extremely* talented. Got the best tables and widest smiles, and potbellied photographers told me I wasn't just *extremely* talented, I was *lovely*. Funny thing, I believed every word. Every single word. Fans surrounded me like fruit flies on a ripe peach.

Why bother with nail polish on my toes? It chips. Chanel Rouge Noir. Love this color. Scrape a few blackish-red flakes onto the flocked carpet. They disappear into the weave. Wonder what else is buried in there.

Ashamed to admit this, but I expected a warm reception since I'm a hometown girl. Thought the concert would sell out, that today would be filled with press appointments. But Madison, whose diplomacy skills lack finesse, told me critics and journalists had no interest. "It's, like, so hard these days to find anyone willing to write about classical music, unless it's, like, some hot new artist. You know, like, the younger ones. I thought, like, since you're older, I might call Walter Wipton."

"Walter Wipton? Is he still on staff at the Pittsburgh paper? My God, that guy has been writing the same shitty review of every young female concert pianist for the last forty years. Is he coming tonight?"

"No," said Madison, checking her phone. "Let's see. He says he already reviewed your performance of the Rachmaninoff."

"That was ten years, ago," I said. "That guy is a sexist idiot. I quote: 'Samantha Lockney might play like a man but she definitely looks like a woman. Sensual and sexy, her body moved with the music and brought to mind moments of passion and release.' Basically, Madison, he compared me to an orgasm. Doesn't get more sexist than that, does it?"

"Wow, you still remember that?" she said. "You're, like, a feminist?"

I didn't know how to answer without shaking her. So I said nothing.

"Well, you know, Baby's in town," said Madison, her voice excited and growing squeakier by the second. "It's supposed to be a secret, but every reporter in Pittsburgh knows she's here. They're all, like, camped out in the lobby. Evidently she's here to attend a funeral."

Fucking Baby. She shows up for a funeral and it's a major press event. I arrive to play the most difficult piano concerto ever written and no one cares.

I pull the covers over my head and try to push away the morning.

Phone rings just as the waiter arrives with my breakfast. Phone tone is an A-natural. Doorbell to the suite is a G-sharp. I'm caught in the crossfire of a half-tone war. God, that's awful. Grab the phone and my robe at the same time.

"Mommy?" It's my daughter, Caroline. Her voice sounds raspy. Make a note to ask Gary if her asthma has been bothering her again. Latrobe isn't far away—should try and get out there to see her. Maybe Gary will bring her to the concert tonight—I already sent tickets. Have to remember to pick up a present—hate to meet her empty-handed. Caroline chatters on about getting ready for school. I look in the mirror and try to iron the lines out of my face with the palm of my hand. Doorbell rings again, followed by loud knocking.

"Yes, sweetie. Yes, sweetie. I miss you, too. Just a minute, okay? Breakfast is here." Fluff my hair and open the door.

Snarky kid with a pierced nose smirks and says, "Room service." These hotel workers get younger every week. His nametag says "Jefferson." Of course. Jefferson. Is every person under the age of twenty-five named after a damn president? Jefferson—wearing a white military jacket with golden buttons and scarlet epaulets and a pair of gravity-defying black pants—slouches into the room without even trying to sneak a peek under my robe. *Pull up your pants,* I want to shout. Little Lord Fauntleroy from the waist up, original gangster from the waist down. Way too skinny for me, anyway. Not tempted.

I don't look bad for my age. I don't. I remind myself of this at least three times an hour. Been playing really well the last few years—playing better than ever, actually—but all the newspapers and magazines want to write about—if they write about me at all—is my puffy face or how much weight I've gained. They say I've "matured in stature." They write about whether I *should* have a face-lift. Or speculate whether I'm losing my hair. If I'm a good mother or a bad mother. If my third marriage will work out. If I'm a lesbian. Downward spiral. Falling face.

To the Jeffersons of the world I am invisible. Rach 3 is too long, too demanding, just too much of everything for a YouTuber like Jefferson. He'll watch a cell phone video of Baby hailing a cab, but an aging formerly-hot classical pianist? Forget it. To music critics—the know-it-alls who fell in love with me when I was waif-like and perky-boobed—I'm one sonata away from menopause. I glance in the mirror as Jefferson rolls the tray table into my suite. Ragged. Chunky. I look my age. And you know what? Just don't care. Really. I don't care.

Enough.

"Where do you want it?" Jefferson says.

"Funny you should ask." I use my flirty voice. Jefferson ignores me. Shit. I remember my ten-year-old daughter is still on the phone, hanging on every word. "Well now, Jefferson, over there. Next to the window." I grab the phone from the nightstand. "Caroline, honey, I'll call you right back, okay?" Already hung up. Guess she has gone to school.

Jefferson, disgusted, places breakfast—a pot of Earl Grey, a bowl of bran flakes, a glass of vivid green juice that will taste like liquid tree—on a window-side table overlooking a broad Pittsburgh avenue. Grant Street? So long since I've been in town. Hardly remember the names of the streets. Jefferson unfurls a single linen napkin, places it next to the tree juice and says, "Will there be anything else?"

"Here." I hand him ten dollars.

"Wow. Thanks," he says.

"You're welcome. Would you perhaps like tickets to my concert this evening? It's not sold out and I have some—"

"What? You a singer or something?"

"No. I'm a concert pianist. I'm performing with the Pittsburgh Symphony this evening."

"Oh. Yeah. I heard of them. But I got plans. I'm not supposed to tell anyone—this is top secret—but I guess you're cool. Baby is in town. I hear she might stop by the Rooster Shack tonight and sit in for a set. At least, that's what my bartender buddy at the Rooster Shack told me."

"Right. Well, then. The Rooster Shack. Imagine that."

"Enjoy your breakfast." Jefferson walks backwards, dragging the empty food cart. He doesn't even glance at me as he backs out of the room.

୬

I eat all of my breakfast. Stroll downstairs, pick up a newspaper. Baby buzz circulates around the reception desk, though she's nowhere to be seen. A grand piano sits right in the middle of the lobby—maybe later I'll challenge Baby to a duel.

Head back to my room. Think about tonight's performance. This damn concerto. Rach 3. I play it really well, but it's never easy. Only a handful of pianists can do it justice. I'm one of them. Pretty much the only thing anyone wants to hear me play these days. It's exhausting keeping up with it. Kicks my ass every time, even after all these years.

Took me *eleven* months to master Rach 3. A "normal" concerto—I can cover that in a month. I remember first looking at the score; it was written for an octopus. No break for the pianist, not even in the second movement. Fell in love with it at eighteen and decided if I never accomplished anything else in my life, I would tame this beast. I did. Now when I play it I become my own orchestra. Two orchestras onstage; the one with eighty-three musicians, and the one behind the Steinway—me. I'm an army, an unbeatable force, a solo musician with the weight of the world balanced on ten fingers. I've sacrificed a lot for Rachmaninoff over the years—childhood, a normal education, several marriages, my daughter, friends—but it's worth it. When I'm playing this concerto, the muscle of the music strong-arms real life. I win. I'm free. I'm home. I'm an unconquerable goddess. I am alive.

Wish I had ordered pancakes or a cheese omelet or something substantial for breakfast. Need real food—potatoes and bread and bacon. If I had a piano in my fucking junior suite I could distract myself with practicing, but the days of the promoter providing a Steinway in my hotel room are over. I look in one of the dozens of mirrors lining the walls. There is a hair growing out of my forehead. My forehead! Jesus Christ, how long has that been there? Oh my God, it's white and it's an inch long. I take a moment and Google cosmetic surgeons in Manhattan. Hair removal, liposuction, Botox, face-lift, fillers—maybe I need a complete rehaul. Might even need an ass lift. No I don't. Yes I do. Not like an ass lift will make me more of an artist. How long would I have to take off from sitting on a piano bench to recover from butt-lift surgery? Forget it. I'm not kowtowing to contemporary beauty standards. Harness my physical well-being to an industry norm? I am what I am, and all that. I pluck the hair.

But maybe if I looked better, if I recaptured my youthful fizz, I would book more gigs. I need to work. I paid off my Manhattan apartment years ago, but I'm so far in debt I'll need to play 150 concerts a year until I'm ninety just to make a dent in what I owe. This is my first gig in a month. I'm not destitute, but I need to pay my staff of anger experts, two ex-husbands, and child support. Maybe there's a direct correlation between weight gain and concert loss. Maybe I'm just too old for this. Not old. Not young. Maybe I'm too fat.

Stop it right now. Just stop it.

I know. Go for a walk. Outside. Fresh air. Breathe. Still have three hours before hair guy shows up. I'll go practice for an hour at the hall. Buy a new dress. Shop for Caroline. What size is she these days? Put on sunglasses and head for Macy's.

Nobody recognizes me in the store, even with sunglasses. Relieved and pissed all at once. I try three separate times to give comp tickets to sales people, but no one seems interested—they act like I'm trying to give them discount coupons for fabric softener. Try on an Oscar de la Renta bright-pink beaded evening gown that costs $2,000. I look like a spangled hippo in a mother-of-the-bride dress, plus the beads chafe my upper arms. Thirty-five minutes of Rach 3 in that thing and my triceps would look like raw meat. Try on a subtle Calvin Klein black sheath dress and I resemble a stout nun settling in for an evening of biblical Scrabble. Try on strappy high-heeled sandals with bits of feathers at the toe. Am I getting cankles? No. Ankles still slim. No ankle lift for me.

How cute! Who ever thought to add feathers to shoes? Could be my new signature style. If Katia Labèque can make a concert pianist fashion statement with red-soled Louboutins, then why not me? Feathers at my feet. Wings on my heels. Fly like an eagle. Buy the shoes. Hope these aren't eagle feathers. Four hundred dollars. Shouldn't, but I do.

I look at a crystal bracelet. Forget that. Pick up a topaz ring for Caroline. Adorable. Topaz is her birthstone, I think. Got to do something about my nails. Looks like I've been digging up potatoes bare-handed.

Scoot down to the cosmetic department and pick up three new lipsticks, a $20 bottle of a nail polish called Cream Cake for my fingers, another bottle of Rouge Noir for my toes, and firming cream guaranteed to restructure a sagging jaw line. Has horse cartilage in it. Or shark fin. Or some awful thing, but *Vogue* says it works.

Hungry. What I eat now is critical. Too much and my stomach will blow up and I'll look five months pregnant onstage and even the feather sandals won't distract from that. If I don't eat enough I'll be shaky, top-heavy, and likely to tip over. Do men think about this shit? No. I'll bet Martha Argerich doesn't either. Should have built my career the way she did.

I find a little Japanese place and order a tempura California roll. Hold the cream cheese. Avocado is good, right? Right. Would kill for some wine, but that's a no-go. I order another California roll. No soy sauce—last thing I need is water retention. There. Full, but not. Perfect.

Over to the hall to see if I can play in these feather sandals. I have my doubts. Piano pedals swallow shoes and long skirts. Test run required. A policeman waves at me. Nice—hey there, big guy. I wave back, but he's not waving at me—he's directing traffic. Pittsburgh pigeon poops on my pink pashmina. I do the best I can to remove the goop with an old Starbucks napkin stuffed in my pocket.

Hands feel cold.

Should have had the wine.

What was I thinking? I'm onstage, running through warm-ups before the technician arrives to tweak the Steinway. Feather sandals are a disaster, heels skid on the wooden floor, I lose control of the pedal. Fuck the feathers. I'm a pianist, not a stripper. I kick them off and keep playing. Stupid idea to buy these stupid shoes. Focus. I should return them, but I'm out of time. Shit. *Focus.* Was I supposed to call Caroline at lunchtime? I'll try later. Help. Stop and clear my head. Play through the cadenza in the first movement again. And again. Again. There. My hands move so fast I can't see or feel them anymore—a blur of sinew and flesh. Part of me, but not. I float above myself, in a trance, listening. Got it now. Stand, stretch, collect my Macy's loot and grab a cab back to the hotel. Time to have hair teased and tussled, face spackled. Salon promised to send someone at four. Could use a piece of cake. Pace back and forth in the suite and wait for hair guy. Think about the Rach. Pace. Stop thinking. Therapist tells me to think of nothing before a performance. Thinking about not thinking. Nothing helps. Keep hearing repetitive patterns in the third movement. Doorbell rings.

Scares me. I'm always jittery a few hours before. It's the stylist, a short guy named Doug. He smells like grapefruit.

"Come in, Doug. May I offer you a *soothing cup of tea?*"

༺༻

Five minutes before eight. Orchestra waits onstage. I wait in the wings. Stretch. Good. Shoulders nice and loose. Hands warm. Neck slightly stiff. Normal. I can see the audience from a gap in the backstage wall. I try not to look. Lots of empty seats. Caroline sits in the third row, with her grandparents and Gary. I'll play the Rach for her tonight. Play it so she'll remember me. The music. Me. The music. Me. The music. Don't think. Don't even think about thinking. The music. Me. Breathe. Believe.

The stage manager taps my shoulder. Walk onstage. Walk. Sit. Maestro raises his baton. The music. Me. Believe. Breathe.

Begin.

The Girl with the Flaxen Hair

An icy breeze hits the back of Baby's neck. Dressed in a dark blue D&G jogging suit, Baby pushes her oversized Chanel sunglasses up on her head. Why, why, are these airports so cold? She yanks the hood over her pale blond hair, slumps into a leather lounge chair, and digs the lacquered nails of her left hand into the padded armrest. With her right hand she holds a mug of green tea.

Baby's real name is Alicia Bonnet, but as a little girl her friends in music class called her Baby Bonnet, and the name stuck. She's flying back home today to attend the funeral of her elementary-school music teacher, Mrs. Melozzi. She has been asked to perform at the memorial service.

"Baby, you need anything?" Baby hates to be bothered, but bothering Baby is Tiffany Ly's job. Tiffany glances at the flight board, looking to see if Baby's flight to Pittsburgh will be leaving on time.

"Nothing," Baby says. "I need nothing." But this is a lie. What Baby really needs right now is a blast of heat, a private plane, a tumbler of Absolut, and a piano. Staring at music notes on her iPad is not going to help her play. She needs to practice. Now. There's no piano in the "Up, Up, and Away" East-West Airlines First Class Lounge. It has been a long time since Baby has been on a commercial flight. But the airport housing her private jet is closed because of some stupid ground-worker's strike, and she has to get back to Pittsburgh today. A rich person's problem. She used to think of Pittsburgh as home, but her few friends have scattered, her sister lives in some awful coal-mining town where she conducts a bell choir—how weird is that?—and her alcoholic mother, whom she hasn't seen for years, works at Meadowbrook, a state home for mentally ill people. As far as Baby is concerned, a mental institution is a perfect place of employment for her stoner mother. She might as well just move in with the rest of the inmates.

Baby used to dream that Mrs. Melozzi was her real mother. "Alicia, sit up straight and curve your fingers," Mrs. Melozzi would say. "Class, watch how Alicia becomes one with the music. She will go far as a musician, as far as she wants to go. Sky high."

"Baby, play some Mozart," the kids used to yell at her.

"Baby, play that Beethoven thing again—the one with the roller-coaster part!"

Mrs. Melozzi made it cool to like classical music. She took large groups of children and taught them how to listen. Some of them—kids with big ears, a cranked-up passion for songs they heard in class, and parents with enough money to pay for private lessons—learned how to play. Mrs. Melozzi, who sensed that Baby was having trouble at home—the whole school had seen her mother stumbling and weaving through city streets on weekend mornings—arranged for private lessons for Baby at Pittsburgh's Center for the Musically Talented, where symphony musicians taught deserving kids classical music and theory.

"Sky high," she would repeat again and again to Baby. "That's how far you can go."

൦ൟ

"You know what?" Baby says to Tiffany, who hovers over her in the airport lounge like a determined urban hummingbird. "If the flight is delayed I want you to call Keith and have him deliver my keyboard."

"Here?"

"Here."

"But—what about security? It's gonna be impossible to get a keyboard past security."

"Make it work. Deal with it. And make sure he brings the new one. Make sure the headphones are with it." Playing a Debussy prelude on a digital keyboard is completely bogus, but Baby has to relearn this composition in the next twenty-four hours or she will be in swampland. Screwing up at Mrs. Melozzi's funeral would be a disaster. People who know about music will be attending the service. And if word gets out that Baby is anywhere near the place, the press will show up.

She pulls up various video performances of the piece on her iPad. Her fingers twitch along with the music.

Baby hasn't played classical music in eight years. Her celebrity—a slinky lace and latex armor she wears with equal amounts of embarrassment and pride—comes from pounding out four chords on a red-lacquered keyboard shaped like a Ferrari. Who needs respectability? She is a one-name celebrity: Madonna, Cher, Pink, Gaga, Baby. Baby plays and sings in stadiums. She shakes her ass. She blasts her fans into rock-induced oblivion. She wears pleather fringe. She knows she is ridiculous, but she can't stop herself.

Baby stares at the iPad and picks at a scaly patch of skin on the palm of her hand. It's like a musician's stigmata—this very spot erupts every time Baby feels a little nervous. Her hand itches, it burns, and sometimes it bleeds. Goddamn Debussy. Why did he have to write complicated music that sounds so simple? All the work, none of the glory. La Fille aux Cheveux de Lin—The Girl with the Flaxen Hair—won't sound good unless it sounds effortless. Effortless takes years. Baby has hours.

"Can I get you a Band-Aid or your special crème, Baby?" asks Tiffany.

"No. I'm fine."

"More tea?"

"No."

Why has Baby agreed to get on a commercial flight, fly across the country in the middle of her tour, and play a piece she couldn't possibly master in the next twenty-four hours? Because she couldn't say no. Not to Mrs. Melozzi's daughter.

"Mother said you once performed a beautiful interpretation of this piece," she said to Baby yesterday on the phone. "When you were in the sixth grade. You know how much she admired your talent."

Baby has twenty years of catch-up practice to do.

"Look, Baby, your flight is leaving on time." Tiffany gestures toward the flight board.

"More green tea, Ms. Baby?" asks the lounge hostess.

Baby looks away.

"We're good," says Tiffany. She flicks her hand at the hostess, brushing her away like a sticky piece of fuzz. She turns back to Baby. "Let's go, Baby. Time to board. I'll call Keith and cancel the keyboard."

"I'm so sorry our first-class ground transportation isn't available for you today," says the hostess. "The President is in town for a fundraiser, and airport vehicles on the field have been restricted."

"What?" says Tiffany. "What? You mean Baby has to *walk*?"

"I'm so sorry, but yes. She'll have to walk through the terminal like everyone else."

"Like, walk *to the plane*?"

"Yes. I'm so sorry."

"That's impossible," says Tiffany. "Baby does *not* walk in public spaces."

"Uh—"

"This is an outrage, a slap in the face to one of America's most beloved entertainers, an insult to performance artists around the world, a—"

"Fuck off, Tiffany," says Baby. "I'm walking. Let's go."

Tiffany and the hostess scurry after Baby, collecting luggage, computer cables, and bits and pieces of things Baby has left behind. The three of them—an unlikely Mod Squad of blond hair, ambition, and black cashmere—step into the main concourse of Terminal D, with two bodyguards flanking them. The first camera flash goes off fifteen feet from the exit to the lounge. It's not one of the usual paparazzi goons, but a civilian with a cell-phone camera, taking the kind of unflattering photo—saggy face, bad posture, mottled skin—that will go viral in about two minutes. How could anyone recognize Baby when she's not wearing full makeup and one of her show costumes? During her current tour she has been sporting a red Louis XIV wig, a mermaid tail, and a bra made entirely out of finger cymbals. Today she's without makeup and wearing the rock-star version of pajamas. No fair. She yanks down her sunglasses, pulls her hood halfway over her face, and hustles, head low, toward the gate.

She hears the whispers.

"Is that her?"

"It is! It's Baby!"

"She looks terrible."

"She looks way too skinny. Is she anorexic?"

"Baby! Baby! Baby!"

"Shit, Tiffany, you said no one knew I was flying commercial," Baby says. "This sucks."

"Sorry, Baby. You're recognizable. It's a good thing. It's full-blown fame. It's what you always wanted. And you have *not* lost weight. *Have you?*"

A stout boy in a Baby hoodie reaches out to touch her. One of the guards shoves him away.

"Jesus Christ," says Baby. By the time she reaches the gate, a crowd has gathered, as if they knew she was arriving. Someone—who?—must have tipped them off. Must have been one of the bodyguards. The crowd applauds and a teenage girl starts to sing the chorus of "Do It Fast."

> *Do it, do it, do it,*
> *Do it real fast,*
> *Do it nice and nasty,*
> *Make the pain last . . .*

Never again. Never again will Baby set foot in a real airport. God, she already has twenty-six full-time employees, and what good is it doing her right now? She pays out over a million dollars a year in salaries to these people. They do her hair, carry her equipment, cook her organic vegan meals, answer her fan mail, prepare her pyrotechnics, clean her toilets, apply her eyeliner, adjust her hemlines, and organize over a hundred concert dates for her each year. But not one of them can help her relearn this piece of piano music. She'll have to do that by herself.

Tiffany escorts Baby to the gate and hands her a piece of Louis Vuitton carry-on luggage, packed with nuts, vitamins, dried fruit, and various silk sleep masks, cashmere scarves, sweaters, gloves and wraps, just in case Baby gets hungry, sleepy, or cold. She shows the flight attendant Baby's ticket and touches Baby on the shoulder. She knows how much Baby hates to be hugged.

"Good luck, Baby. It's all good. I'm sorry I can't travel with you, but I need to be in New York preparing for your show. Jimbo is flying with you today and will stay next door to you in Pittsburgh."

"Jimbo?"

"Jimbo, your favorite guard? The guy with the rhino tattoo?"

"Right. Jimbo."

"Text if you need anything. I'll catch up with you in Manhattan on Tuesday. Madison Square is sold out—good news, right?—and we'll be ready for you when you arrive for the sound check. Nine o'clock leave time. Jimbo has the schedule—don't worry about a thing. A Steinway B has been delivered to your suite at the William

Penn Hotel—you have the Governor's suite. Your code name at the hotel is Clarissa Ratalinski."

"*Clarissa Ratalinski*? That's awful."

"Uh, it's my mother's maiden name. I thought it sounded kind of Pittsburgh-y."

"Oh. Look, Tiff, I'm sorry. I can be a real asshole sometimes. Not to make excuses, but I guess I'm pretty shaken up about Mrs. Melozzi and the funeral, and, you know, about going back home."

Tiffany smiles at Baby. She gets paid to listen to Baby's apologies and excuses. "No problem, Baby! I completely understand. I know this is a very sad time for you. And anyway, forget about Pittsburgh—New York City has always been your real home. And you have your musical family—"

Baby holds up her hand as if to say STOP. Tiffany is not her friend; she's just another employee.

"Okay. You'll have a few hours to practice when you get in. You can have an early dinner and get to bed at a decent time. Ambien is in your drug and vitamin kit, like always. Funeral service is tomorrow morning at 11:00. Oh, I've FedEx'd your black Versace suit. A stylist will show up at the hotel in the morning. Safe travels!"

Baby wonders for a second if she really needs a stylist to attend a funeral. Of course she does. She's Baby.

Baby steps into the long narrow jetway leading to the plane that will carry her back to Pittsburgh. The other passengers have already boarded. Even though Jimbo skulks behind her, Baby feels alone. She stops for a moment in the grim tunnel with the curved and grimy eggshell-colored walls, wondering what would happen if she plopped down on the gummy blue carpeting and cried. But Baby doesn't stop moving. She walks faster and faster, rushing, finally racing toward her seat on the plane.

She enters the first-class section, sits in the beige vinyl seat, and breathes. Jimbo settles in across the aisle from her.

"May I get you anything, Ms. Baby?" asks the flight attendant. "A glass of champagne, perhaps?"

Baby looks out the window at the orange-suited men on the ground loading huge crates of something into the broad belly of the jet. She glances back at the flight attendant. "You don't have a piano on board, do you?" Baby says. The flight attendant looks dazzled, as if she wants to snap her fingers and conjure one out of the tinny airplane air.

"It's a joke," says Baby. "It's just a joke." Baby breathes. Again. Once more.

"A glass of water will be fine," Baby says. "No ice. Two slices of lime."

"Here you are, Ms. Baby," says the flight attendant as she hands Baby her beverage. "Cheers! I know you'll be happy to get back home."

The plane begins to taxi. Home is home. This sounds like a song lyric, except nothing good at all rhymes with home—*foam, dome, roam, gnome*. Fact is, the only good rhyme for home is, well, *home*. It's not very poetic, but it's still the best choice.

Baby likes writing songs on airplanes. She pulls out her iPad.

"This is your captain speaking. We've reached a cruising altitude of 35,000 feet."

"Sky high," Baby types onto the blank screen. "Sky high."

༄

The music, once she practiced for several hours in her suite, came back to her fingers quickly enough. Up since dawn, Baby played through the Debussy enough times to know she won't screw up, at least not in a way anyone will notice.

At ten o'clock, appropriately coiffed and decked out in Versace funeral black, Baby leaves the hotel with Jimbo and a driver, clutching the Debussy sheet music in a sleek black folder under one arm. Tiffany has thought of everything, even a Vuitton music portfolio to match her shoes—spiky black heels with dark feathers attached to the toes. The lobby swarms with photographers as she makes her way to the car. Jesus, will the church let these bloodsuckers inside? She hopes not.

Baby asks the driver to stop for a moment on Grandview Avenue, at an overlook that clings like a large mushroom to the side of Mt. Washington. She has always loved this view. Two rivers meet and make a third, almost like a family. As a little girl Baby used to perch up here, snug against a protective railing, and dream about swooping over the side of the mountain, past the bling of the mirrored skyscrapers, wondering if she might see herself reflected in the steely skyline. Today she wishes the wind could cradle her in its sinewy December limbs, sweep her over the golden triangle, and carry her past the saw-toothed horizon, along the mighty Ohio River, and into her mother's scrawny embrace.

She blinks and turns away from the city, checks to see if the bench where she once carved her name is still there—it is—and walks towards the church.

"Baby, Ms. Baby!" says Jimbo. "Where are you going?"

"To the church," Baby says. "It's just a block away."

"But you can't walk," says the guard.

"Watch me," says Baby. "I'm walking. Keep up with me if you can."

Baby reaches the front door of the church. With Jimbo's help, she nudges her way through a mess of press people crowded behind a velvet rope at the entrance. A church worker greets her. Baby enters the sanctuary. Something's not right. Only thirty or forty people have bothered to come. It's still early. Baby nods at Mrs. Melozzi's daughter and finds the seat reserved for her. Her name, Alicia Bonnet, has been written in black Magic Marker on a small sign taped to the back of the pew. The church smells musty.

Tomorrow night Baby will perform a sold-out concert at Madison Square Garden. This morning she will play a funeral for a half-empty house in a town she always hated. What the fuck?

She has come to say thank you and goodbye. Baby isn't good at that, but she hopes Debussy will help her out. The stained-glass windows, dark and dull in the tilted winter light, bathe the church in shades of purple, green, and blue. The closed coffin rests next to the piano. Baby wonders if dead music teachers can still hear mistakes. She hopes Mrs. Melozzi hears how Baby becomes one with the music.

Together the congregation sings "A Mighty Fortress Is Our God." The minister reads Scripture: "With nothing I came out of my mother's body, and with nothing I will go back there; the Lord gave and the Lord has taken away; let the Lord's name be praised."

The church feels cold, as churches do. Too much stone.

"Alicia Bonnet will now play Debussy's Girl with the Flaxen Hair, one of Crystal Melozzi's favorite compositions."

Baby rises and walks to the piano. As hard as she tries, she cannot steady her shaking hands.

Song for Alice

Gary Lee Love throws his gig bag over his shoulder. He doesn't like to leave the guitar unattended in a parked car—it's exactly the kind of thing a hard-up junkie would steal. He slams the trunk of his mom's champagne-beige Toyota Camry. It's a classic old-lady car if he's ever seen one, but Gary is happy to have wheels and even happier to be out of his parents' house. It's ten in the morning and he's making his way to a "Sing Along with Gary" gig at the Mount Royal Senior Citizens Center in downtown Latrobe. The job starts at one, but Gary has stopped here, at the Latrobe Civic Center, to attend a morning meeting of Alcoholics Anonymous. Gary has a firm rule, one that has kept him sober for the last fourteen years: Never ever play a job without attending a meeting first. It's not always easy to find a meeting at the right time, but this is his rule and he sticks to it. No meeting, no gig.

Gary plays every other week at Mount Royal—the alternate week is covered by a sweet girl from Beaverdale, an accordion player named Bluesette. He has never met Bluesette in person, but she sounds real nice on the phone. Gary has been to this particular AA meeting many times, because it's the only one in a fifty-mile radius that starts early enough for him to make a lunchtime job. Attendance at the meeting has slipped in recent months—most of the regulars have either relapsed or gotten jobs that require them to show up during business hours. But Gary knows he can count on a few familiar faces this morning. It's an unusually bright day—crisp November air, almost crunchy, and he breathes deeply as he climbs the steps to the Civic Center. It still feels good to have a clear head. Gary opens the sparkling glass door and walks to the meeting room at the back of the first floor. He can smell brewing coffee and cigarette smoke before he even enters the room.

"Morning, Gary!"

"Morning, Alice." Gary hugs Alice and draws back to look at her little walnut face. She has snowy white hair and smells like cinnamon. Alice likes to bake. She doesn't have many teeth, but that doesn't stop her from smiling. Gary doesn't know much about Alice—just that she works as a nurse's aide at a place called Meadowbrook, a state mental institution in Pittsburgh. He wonders about Alice's age. She could be anywhere between forty-five and seventy. Addiction is funny like that—it takes a person's features and jumbles them around, distills the decades, and decants what's yet to come.

Alice tugs on the strap of Gary's gig bag. Her hands are knobby and hard. "One of these days you have to play for us, darlin'."

"You ply me with enough of those apple fritters, Miss Alice, and you'll get more out of me than just a song."

Alice blushes and turns away to arrange her fritters on paper plates. There are enough fritters to feed twenty-five, even though there are only four people in the room. Two beefy men, Buck and Duane, slurp hot coffee from Styrofoam cups. Gary recently discovered they are brothers. They both wear camouflage jackets, blaze-orange vests, and caps with laminated hunting licenses pinned on them. Deer season started yesterday. Gary doesn't understand why anyone would hunt. And it freaks him out to think of recovering alcoholics stomping through the woods with shotguns. He's no better than Duane and Buck, but at least his weapon of choice is a guitar, which—most of the time—is pretty harmless.

Gary tries to start a little chit-chat, but he's never sure what to say to these guys. He guesses they feel the same way about him. "Shoot anything yesterday?" he asks Duane.

"Six-pointer. Got enough meat for the winter now. But that animal put up one hell of a fight. Tracked him for a solid two miles before he fell. It was a bitch draggin' him back to the truck."

"I didn't have as much luck," says Buck. "Stayed out in the woods for six hours freezing my butt off—never saw a thing. Nothin' was moving out there; damn forest looked like an oil painting. Should we get started with the meeting?"

"Yep. Good idea," says Gary as he pulls up two chairs, one for him and one for his guitar. Buck stands behind a lectern.

"My name is Buck and I'm an alcoholic."

"Hi, Buck," says everyone.

"Hi."

"First order of business: Attendance at last week's meeting was three. Pretty much the same as this week's meeting, except today we have Gary. So that makes four."

"Anything we can do to increase attendance?" asks Duane. "Like maybe have the meeting at a time when people can actually *come*?"

"Protocol, Duane."

"Right. Sorry. My name is Duane and I'm an alcoholic."

"Hi, Duane.

"Hi. Like I said. Anything we can do to increase attendance?"

"Well," says Buck. "We can't actually go out on the street and haul people in here. Especially during hunting season. But we do know there are a lot of drunks in downtown Latrobe."

"I have an idea," says Gary.

"Protocol, please."

"My name is Gary and I'm an alcoholic."

"Hi, Gary."

"Hi. Maybe we need to do some marketing. Posters or something. Email? A Facebook fan page? A benefit concert?"

"Thank you, Gary," says Buck. "I'll make a note of that for the next meeting. And now, it's time for the General Secretary's report." Buck is the General Secretary as well as the Chairperson. He shuffles through some papers. "Hi. I'm Buck and I'm still an alcoholic."

"Hi, Buck."

"Hi. Uh, no report from the General Secretary. So let's move on to sharing and discussion. Anyone want to open up the discussion?"

"Yes," says Alice. Alice hardly ever speaks at meetings. The three men turn their heads in her direction.

"Protocol, Alice."

"My name is Alice and I'm an alcoholic."

"Hi, Alice."

"Hi. I have been recovering for fifteen years. But last Saturday, I felt the need to drink. I actually bought a bottle of Maker's Mark and set it right down on my kitchen table. I stared at it for a while. It was *calling* me."

"What happened, Alice?" asks Buck. "What happened to make you want to drink?"

"Nothing, really. I was just bored. Missing my daughters, don't you know. One of them travels a lot and hasn't talked to me for years. The other one found God and dropped out of my life. I'm sort of sad, I guess. Living alone, heating up those goddamn soup-for-one things, watching the way the ground gets sludgy and the air loses its color this time of year. It gets tiresome. That's all. Just tiresome. I hate November and I hate low-sodium lentil soup. And I wanted a goddamn drink. Is that so awful? I guess it is for me. One's too many; fifty's not enough. I tried to call my sponsor, but I got her answering machine. I think she might be drinking again. Or using. If anything can set a gal off, it's November and that goddamn soup."

"*Did* you drink, Alice?"

"No, sir. I did *not*. I decided to turn on the radio, you know, just to distract myself a bit. But I kept starin' at that damn bottle of bourbon."

"Whoa," says Duane. "That's intense."

"Right," says Alice. "Right. It was intense. But then this song came on. Something called 'November Morning.' Kind of sappy and cliché, you know. Mushy. But the guy singing it got to me. It was about, I don't know, crumpled leaves and blue frost and the way everything *seems* to die in the fall, but how it doesn't die, not really, it just gets buried and smothered by cold and ice and big old sheets of nothingness. Some shit like that. And you know what I thought? I thought, well that's what drinking does to me. It freezes my brain and makes me kind of dead, even though I'm not. Not really. And I thought, well, I don't want to be dead or even half-dead. If I'm dead, I won't be able to hear music or make apple fritters or see the sun when its sorry ass finally shows itself in Latrobe. Like today. Did you notice? You can see yourself if you look up—that's how clean the sky is."

"Whoa," says Duane. "That's, like, poetry."

"Yeah, yeah," says Alice. "But that stupid song saved me. I kept the plug in the jug, so to speak. I listened to find out who the singer was, but they didn't say. Those radio people never say anything I want to hear."

Gary cannot breathe. "November Sky." He doesn't know whether to confess or not. He wrote and recorded that song back in 1992 when he was the golden boy of folk-rock—before his first rehab; before he fell in love with opiates and vodka and anything he could snort; before his concert-pianist wife got famous, ditched him for a tour of Europe, and left him alone to raise their daughter; before he left Manhattan and spent all his money on crystal meth and street versions of prescription drugs; before he wasted five years in jail after getting busted for forging checks; long before he attended his second, third, and fourth rehabs; before he and Caroline moved in with his eighty-year-old parents because they didn't have anywhere else to go.

Gary Lee Love wrote the song before he knew the score—before he knew that music could help people like Alice. Had he known, he might have saved himself fifteen years of crumpled leaves and blue frost. He might have picked up his Gibson and done some good with it. Maybe there was still time.

Buck, Alice, and Duane don't know Gary's last name. They don't know he was once a rising star or a falling star or any kind of star at all. They know he's a musician and an alcoholic who plays sing-along sessions for the aging citizens of Latrobe, and that's about it. His baldness and midlife paunch pretty much guarantee his anonymity. He decides, in the amount of time it takes to play a grace note, to give this moment to the new Gary. "I'm sorry," he says, glancing at his watch. "I have to go to work. Don't wanna be late for my concert."

"Grab a couple of fritters on the way out," says Alice. "And next time, I wanna hear that song you keep promising me."

"Wait," says Buck. "Protocol. We gotta do the Serenity Prayer."

"All right," says Gary. He hates the Serenity Prayer. It sounds like the lyric to a bad country song. But Gary follows the rules because it's the only way he can get from here to there and back again. Who needs bluish frost, anyway?

The four recovering alcoholics join hands and lower their heads. The laminated plastic of Duane's hunting license—pinned to the top of his cap—reflects the glare of the overhead fluorescent lights. The badge looks like a miner's light, an inefficient blob of brightness in a bleak world.

God, grant me the serenity to accept the things I cannot change, the courage to change the things I can, and the wisdom to know the difference.

Gary, feeling not very wise and not very brave, but more serene than he did when he arrived at the meeting, picks up his gig bag, wraps a couple of fritters in a paper napkin, nods to Alice, Buck, and Duane, and leaves to go play his program for the old folks.

Hungry

Amelie Neeson carries her cello through the parched parking lot in front of the Meadowbrook County Home in Chestnut Ridge, Pennsylvania. Her string quartet, Viva!, a group she put together three years ago—with the goal of playing in small concert halls and chamber music venues—hasn't had many bookings lately. This week she's grateful to have one job: a Musician's Union Trust Fund gig in a state mental institution.

Meadowbrook is a nice name for a forlorn residence. Neither meadow nor brook graces the urban landscape. Swollen chestnut trees salute Meadowbrook's entrance like sullen sentries guarding a run-down French palace. To Amelie the hard-boiled summer air tastes vaguely metallic. Rusty, almost. Overcooked yellow rose bushes climb the glazed brick gateway, and a sad sprinkler system spits tepid water on the roasted August lawn. Amelie has been here before. She already imagines the smells of urine and grease, the vague scents of pears and disinfectant. She can also smell her mother's shampoo.

Amelie perches on the front steps, her cello case snuggled in the sweaty crook of her arm, and scans the scalded horizon for signs of her colleagues. She canceled three students today to make this concert. She hates Trust Fund gigs, especially in this place, but often they provide the only work she can get as a performer. Last time she played here, six months ago, a man the attendants called "Jockey" spent the duration of the Mozart String Quartet No. 19 in C major circling Amelie on an imaginary pony while yelling "off to the races." Another patient, a woman named Becky, handed Amelie a peeled banana and asked her to hide it in her cello case. One thing Amelie has learned about working at Meadowbrook: never leave an instrument unattended. And never, ever lose sight of the bow.

"Hey, Amelie," says Tom the violinist as he climbs out of his van. Tom has broad shoulders, a winning smile, and bad dandruff. "The others here yet?"

"No," says Amelie. "But it's too hot to wait outside. Let's go in. At least they have air conditioning."

"Okay. Will your mother be here today?"

"She has been here for twenty years, Tom. I doubt she packed her bags and moved to Bermuda."

"I mean in the audience, if you can call it that. Will she be one of the inmates in the audience?"

"Of course," says Amelie. "She loves Mozart. And they're called *patients*, Tom, not inmates."

༄

Amelie places her purse, belt, cell phone, and dangling earrings in a gray plastic tray and hands it to Mr. Joyce, a withered security guard with a goat-like face. For as long as Amelie has been visiting her mother, Mr. Joyce has been checking her in. And out.

"Afternoon, Ms. Neeson," he says, stroking his pointy white beard. "Lucky us—an afternoon of your fine music."

"Always a pleasure to play here, Mr. Joyce! You remember Tom, our violinist? The other two musicians will be here soon."

"You and Tom go on ahead. You know the lay of the land around here. I'll escort the others when they arrive. Saw your mother at breakfast, by the way. She was telling everyone about the concert today. You're a Meadowbrook celebrity. Is it true you played at Carnegie Hall when you were five?"

"No."

"Didn't think so. Well. You know how she likes to brag. Typical mother."

"Typical?"

"Sort of. You all have a nice performance."

༄

Amelie was a typical five-year-old girl when her mother, Susan, committed the crime that landed her in a state penitentiary, and eventually Meadowbrook. Susan—a capable single mother and a rising star on the Pittsburgh culinary scene—attacked a customer who complained about the vinaigrette on her minced-duck-breast salad. Susan never drank anything more than the occasional chef's glass of Sancerre. She seemed completely sober and sane at the time—a little overworked maybe, a little tired. But when a waiter told her that the lady at table five said there was "too much honey in the salad dressing," she flew into a rage, raced out of the kitchen with her best filet knife, and stabbed the complaining woman in the neck. The woman, it turned out, was the mayor's wife.

"*Excusez moi*, you stupid asshole. It's *not* honey," Susan shouted at the First Lady of Pittsburgh. "It's pear purée, you whining nitwit. *Purée de poire.*" She screamed at the other customers, upturned several tables, and threw a potted plant at the cashier before anyone could restrain her.

Susan's attorney, Bernie "Call me Bernard" Steeb, had a hard time defending Susan, especially since there were almost thirty witnesses, most of whom left the restaurant shaken and nauseated, but happy they had not ordered the *canard hachées*. It was a sorry joke in Pittsburgh for a while. *Whatever you do, don't order the duck.* The D.A charged Susan with aggravated assault and attempted murder. To save her from an unsavory prison term, Bernie persuaded Susan to cop an insanity plea, which seemed a reasonable tactic since normal chefs, *typical* chefs, in spite of their reputation for being temperamental, usually don't stab diners in the neck with a filet knife.

When Bernie's team investigated Susan's past, they discovered clear signs that she had been teetering on the edge of a nervous breakdown. She had shaved her head, she smelled like bouillabaisse, and, as she stood for hours over the stovetop—testing and tasting, kneading and frothing—she cursed invisible demons and waved herb-filled paper bags to chase them away. Someone should have tried to help, but her employees feared her wrath, customers found her charmingly eccentric, and her family—who hardly ever saw her—attributed Susan's behavior to her artist's temperament.

Susan served ten years in the Waymar State Prison. While there, the good doctors in the psychiatric division discovered she was truly mentally ill. Upon her release, doctors recommended her transfer to a state mental institution. So now, Susan Neeson, The Attack Chef—as the Pittsburgh Post-Gazette once called her—lives in Meadowbrook, mixed up and medicated; choking down corned-beef hash and lime Jell-O in the dining room. Sometimes she remembers she's a mother. Sometimes not.

After Susan went to prison, little Amelie lived with her Aunt Cathy in Cleveland. An investment banker with lots of money and loads of love, Cathy had absolutely no interest in pear purée. A single woman, she had always wanted a child. Everyone, it seemed, got something from Susan's ordeal except for Susan herself. Amelie got Aunt Cathy and a really expensive cello, Aunt Cathy got a cute and talented adopted daughter, Mrs. Mayor got a triple strand of pearls to camouflage the scar on her neck, Mr. Mayor got a second, third, and fourth term (nothing like a stabbing incident to gain sympathy votes), and Bernie got paid. Quite a chain of events for an incident that began with vinaigrette.

Susan's release from Meadowbrook will never happen. Everyone, even Susan, knows this. According to the experts, her type of schizophrenia—combined with a severe form of conduct disorder—often leads to violent behavior. "Without medication and observation, anything could happen," Aunt Cathy says.

The idea that *anything could happen* excites Amelie, just a little. She was almost sixteen before Aunt Cathy told her the truth about Susan. How was she supposed to feel about having a mother in a mental institution? She didn't feel deserted or sad or empty or ashamed. She didn't feel anything at all. She kept doing what she had been doing since the day she arrived at Aunt Cathy's house. She played the cello. She practiced and listened and practiced some more because she loved music and couldn't think of anything better to do with herself. Like her mother, she learned a craft, a skill, a technique.

By the time Amelie finally visited her mother for the first time, Susan had been in Meadowbrook for two years. The meeting was awkward, with Aunt Cathy forcing conversation. Music and food, music and food, nothing to talk about but music and food.

Amelie never admitted it, but she liked having a mom in an institution. She thought it gave her an adolescent edge. Most teenage girls think their mothers are crazy; Amelie's mother was the real deal. Mom, interrupted, with recipes. Intrigued by Susan's drama,

Amelie wondered if someday she, too, might snap. She even *tried* to hear voices in her everyday life—trilling angels, growling devils, anything but the weighty stillness and boredom that contained her. As she grew older and began to play with various ensembles, she began to hear the sonorous tone of her cello talking to her. Through her cello she heard voices—stern declarations from weeping children or whispered secrets from lost generations. When she played, she also heard the soaring melodies she had missed as a child, harmonic underpinnings that lifted her above herself, a circular wall of sound that protected her from places like Meadowbrook. Sometimes, when she subbed with the Pittsburgh Symphony or played a quartet concert in a beautiful venue, she would stand with her colleagues, listen to applause, exit the concert hall, go home, eat a peanut butter sandwich, and celebrate and mourn her normal life.

She most likely hadn't inherited her mother's disease, nor—and this she realized later with both relief and disappointment—had she inherited her talent. Susan had been an illustrious chef, one of a kind. Amelie was a section cellist, a typical cellist, one of many. Skilled, but not unique. Proficient, but not magical. She would never be a star; she would never be crazy. She would do her job, make beautiful music, and live a quiet life. In her early twenties she moved to Manhattan with the dream of starting a solo career, but she felt lost there, untethered, abandoned. She returned to Western Pennsylvania, took an adjunct teaching position at a local college, and visited Susan whenever she found time. She knew where she belonged: somewhere close to her mother, but not too close.

Today, when Amelie steps into the Meadowbrook community lounge, she spots Susan immediately, perched on a no-color sofa, alert and wearing a blueberry-blue jogging suit with pinkberry-pink stripes. Her hair, once auburn and ropey, is now sizzling white and flyaway, as if she has taken a whisk to it.

Susan's eyes swivel to Amelie as she steps into the room.

"Hello, Mother! You've done something to your hair. It looks festive. Like a meringue. Very nice!"

"Hello, Amelie. Hello." They lean toward each other, but neither woman reaches for the other. No hugs, no handshakes, no pats on the back. They both like it this way.

"Hello, Mrs. Neeson," says Tom.

"Mother, you remember my friend Tom, the violinist?"

"Of course I remember," says Susan. "Tom, do you know that tobacco and cabbage grow side by side in the same field?"

"Do they now?" says Tom. "I'll go set up, Amelie, so you can have a few minutes with your mother."

"STAY AWAY FROM ED!" shouts Susan.

"Who is Ed?" says Tom. "He's not that jockey guy, is he?"

"The man with the freckles and the flamingo-print pants," says Susan, suddenly whispering. "He's crazy. He thinks he can sing. But he only knows one song—'Climb Every Mountain.' He'll sing it and never stop if he thinks someone is listening."

Susan has gotten thinner. Her skin is translucent, see-through almost, and her fingers have grown knobby, like thick stalks of ginger root. Doctors say medication extinguishes the fire in patients like Susan, but today her eyes throw dangerous embers in all directions.

Amelie hears a hum, a buzz, an odd hiss in the room that sounds like a simmering pot of soup.

"It's the first rule of running a restaurant," says Susan in a monotone voice, laced with the opposite of syrup—salt maybe, or something bitter. "You cannot poison your guests."

"What are you talking about, Mother?"

"The food here. She's trying to poison us."

"Who, Mother?"

"Debbie. That crazy chef. Back there. In that inferno. The kitchen. She will kill us all. You cannot poison your guests. You cannot. It's against the rules."

"But, Mother—"

"Let's not bring that old story up *again*."

"Okay. I wasn't—"

"I can't blame her, I can't. She spends too much time caramelizing and basting and boiling and baking. Sauté, stew, smoke, and sweat. It drives us all mad. Mad. Mad."

"Mother," Amelie says. "Debbie doesn't want to hurt you."

"You haven't tried her Waldorf salad. If you had you would know she's out to get me. Maybe she's jealous."

"Of what?"

"Of me. She knows I'm the competition."

"But you haven't cooked in twenty years. I'm sure Debbie the chef doesn't even know who you are." Amelie says this without thinking, and for a moment she's afraid Susan might cry.

"Still. I'm watchful. I've been observing the other guests, to see if any of them drop dead. The chicken potpie looks suspicious to me. And Mr. Barney started sniveling and hacking today at lunch, right after he ate the creamed carrots. YOU TELL ME THAT'S NOT A COINCIDENCE."

"Mother, please, no need to yell."

"You're right. I should just play along with the whole thing. If they know I suspect Debbie, the jig is up. And then they'll get me. Anyway, I'm tired. And hungry." Susan crumples into the sofa. It almost swallows her.

"Have you been eating?"

"No. I give my food away. To the other guests. They are my tasters, my testers. Like a queen. I have people who test my food for me. Like a queen. Like a queen." She closes her eyes and begins to hum a song with no melody.

Amelie hopes today's concert will soothe Susan. "Shall I play for you, Mother?"

"Yes. You play the cello the way I cook," says Susan, cracking open one eye. "Like you're always searching for the right flavor, the essence, like you're always trying to get it right. Play for me, sweetheart. See if one time you can get it right. I never could."

"And if I don't?"

"Oh, you won't. But you'll keep trying."

"Yes. I will."

"Two dollars, please. That will be two dollars. Two dollar cover charge." Sissy, a new patient at Meadowbrook, sits at a tiny desk and tries to charge patients for admission to the concert. Amelie stares in disbelief as they file in and go through the motions of paying Sissy. One by one they reach into nonexistent pockets and handbags, grab a handful of air, and place it on Sissy's desk.

"I refuse to pay the cover charge," says Susan. "She's up to no good with that money. I'm not paying a cover charge to hear Mozart in a nut house. Plus, you know, I already have reserved seating. You're my daughter, after all. That means I'm special."

Alice, a nurse's aid, offers a plate of warm cookies to Susan .

"No, thank you, Alice," says Susan, waving away the plate. "I'm not hungry. I used to be. But not now. Not any longer."

"Okay, Susan," says Alice. "But sooner or later you'll have to eat something. Lucky you—a visit today from your daughter! More Mozart today? I hope so. We always love when you play for us, don't we Susan? Don't we love it when she plays?"

"Maybe we do," says Susan. "Maybe we don't."

"My daughters are both musicians," says Alice. "I would give anything to hear them. But we have lost touch."

Amelie, who is starving, grabs a cookie and puts it in her pocket for later. These days, she is always famished. She has run out of things to say, so she waves at Susan, walks toward the makeshift stage, and joins Tom. Lila and Stan have arrived, and the four of them arrange their stands, tune up, and organize their music.

Amelie holds the bow above the strings, closes her eyes, and tries to focus. In spite of everything—Jockey, the cover-charge conspiracy, the unmistakable sounds of "Climb Every Mountain" echoing from a nearby corridor—she will discover little pieces of herself today. Where thoughts fail, music takes over, cramming unspoken wishes into silence, filling empty space with desire, satisfying minor cravings with hope.

Amelie listens to her cello, forgets where she comes from, and faces the world. It's that simple.

Manhattan Road Trip

Welcome to Manhattan! You can call me Manny. Nice to meet you. I know, I know—in spite of the Armani cologne, I don't smell so great. No time to shower today. It's not easy sharing a chunk of land with a million and a half people and no water pressure. And the noise. God. Too many musicians. I stopped this morning to listen to an alto sax player practicing a hip version of "Nature Boy." Gorgeous—and, well, the next thing I knew it was noon. Time for the daily *meet and greet*. So. Here I am. Hello! Yes. It's loud here, isn't it? Music, music, everywhere. I love it, I hate it. Playing, playing on the streets and the piers, in the clubs and the halls and the subways. Singing, swinging, honking, plucking, pounding. It used to be the land of the free. Now it's the land of free music. Seems like the only thing we pay for these days is silence.

Greetings, my friends! Tell me your names. Rosie? Matthew? Attila? Nice. Welcome, to all of you. Yeah, go ahead and look up. That's what I did when I first arrived. I planted my swollen feet on the steamy sidewalk, looked at a slice of sky, and wondered why so many buildings were made of mirrors. Speaking of which—Rosie? You might want to check your lipstick—you got some on your teeth. Not a good look.

I used to be a musician. I played the piano. I wrote songs. Good songs. I gave it up long ago. Between us, I kind of regret it.

I was good enough to make it here. I was. I had a few jobs playing rehearsals for Off-Broadway musicals. I even subbed once on *Little Shop of Horrors*. But the guys in the suits nabbed me—said I had management potential—and made me the Voice of Manhattan. And you can't be the Voice of Manhattan and a composer at the same time. Trust me, I tried. If you have to pick between the two, well, being the Voice of Manhattan is easier than playing the piano. Fringe benefits, sick pay. The food is pretty good and you can't beat the real estate. I miss playing, though. I even miss the singers. But it's my own damn fault for quitting. I turned forty, real life got too complicated, and I decided to go for the money job. I checked out and cashed in. But I'm happy. I really am happy. Happy, happy, happy. Hey, you heard Hank Staples lately? He's got the happy-hour piano gig over at the Waldorf. Got a mean left hand, but he won't last long. I hear they want to hire a harpist.

So here *you* are, another skilled musician shuffling onto my shores, reminding me of who I used to be. You're competent. Strong. Dedicated and infatuated with the art of playing. *What?* You say you're here because your musical path, your spiritual journey, your *personal road* led you to *me?*

Oh, I see. You're a poet, too. Very, very nice. But what's all this nonsense about roads? Roads are for small-town wimps. Who needs them? You're in New York City now, so buck up! We got bulging streets and macho avenues that crisscross concrete corridors; throbbing big-city blocks that pulse in time to whatever tune you're playing. You like that, don't you? I know your type. You're not scared. You're gutsy and bold and ready to take on anything I throw at you—a minimum-wage survival gig, an apartment infested with giant bugs that don't exist in your hometown, a landlord who won't let you practice, a diet of peanut butter and air. Nothing will keep you from your music, not even alternate-side-of-the-street parking.

Squawk at me—go ahead. Blow your horn on Sixth Avenue or whistle a tune next to the Hudson. But step lively, would you please? And don't block the box. I got a sore throat and I don't want to yell at you.

Forgive me. I'm the voice of the city that never sleeps and sometimes I'm a little cranky. I talk a lot but I can't stop listening. How can anyone catch a nap when there's so much going on? That guy over on Forty-eighth Street who plays the trombone? He won't stop practicing. He's so good it makes me weep. Weep! I guess he's the way I used to be, the way you are now. You know, unyielding, determined to make a mark, stupid.

You don't know much about being cranky, do you? You're from Tahoe or Toledo or Turtle Creek. You have *talent*. You're *hopeful*. Nothing has ever gone wrong in your privileged life. You're bright-eyed and bubble-faced when you plop onto the grid. With two fierce legs and the luck of the guileless—you remind me a little of my half-witted cousin Angela—I mean that in a good way—you land firmly in my territory without missing a beat. You're one of many. Hundreds of you, arriving every week, jumping on the island's spine. You're like wingless fleas, flitting around looking for places to play, to practice. I respect you, but your efforts exhaust me. You hardly stop to eat. You're young. I spit at you, just to show you who's in charge. You zig, you zag, you rush, you drag. Soon, if you're not careful, you're lost inside *my* song, a little ditty I've been humming for way too long. It's a drone, really. A zombie chorus, with percussion. It's the last thing I wrote before I quit, so it's a little on the angry side. I try to throw you off course with my monotone voice and a snap of my gnarled fingers. But you ignore me. Your belief in yourself is steadfast, solid as the leftover glacial rock formations in Central Park. By the way, it's worth mentioning that hundreds of people injure themselves on those rocks every year. Not that you'll be one of them. Not you.

Warning: It's my job to break you. Just thought you ought to know. See, there's only so much space here for musicians, artists, actors, writers. I'm the guy—the show-biz vigilante—who tries to convince you to leave. I work on commission so I'm very motivated. I can't mess with your music—I know better than that—but I can mess with your head. I'll insult you, tear you down, dash your hopes, mash your faith. It's a nasty way to make a living. But I've always been a bit of a narcissistic bully, so it comes naturally to me. And hey, I have to pay my rent, too. Just like you. Difference is, I have a steady paycheck.

Maybe you're shocked that I'm a man. So many artists think Manhattan is a woman—that whole gender-bending Lady Liberty thing has you confused. You like to think that once you're here, a statuesque woman in a flowing robe will look after you. Like she cares. Lady Liberty—I know her from way back—is tone deaf. She hates music. I heard her try to sing "My Funny Valentine" one time at a door gig over in Fort Lee. I guess she figured if everyone else was singing it, she might as well give it a try. She got to that "stay little Valentine" part, and really, I thought my head would explode. Anyway, if you think Lady Liberty—whose real name is Claudette, by the way—is on your side, think again. Claudette is pissed, she's green, and she's going nowhere fast. And let's not forget those spikes on her crown. Ah, French humor.

Give me your tired, your poor, your huddled masses yearning to breathe free, the wretched refuse of your teeming shore. Send these, the homeless, tempest-tossed, to me: I lift my lamp beside the golden door.

See, that would be you—the huddled masses. I don't know if Emma Lazarus was thinking of second violinists, heavy-metal guitarists, or warbling singer-songwriters when she wrote that little snippet, but it kind of applies.

Lunch!

So what do you want with your tempest-tossed salad at The Golden Door Deli? A turkey sandwich on rye with spicy mustard? That's easy, if you've got six bucks. A skyline view? A walk across the Brooklyn Bridge while someone quotes Walt Whitman? No problem. But I think you want more. You're looking for fame, fortune, a career in the performing arts, right? Maybe all you want is respect. Or maybe you want to express your feelings and *connect* with people while you do it. You think you've got something to say with your music.

Give me a break.

I don't care how good you are, how many goddamn Scriabin Preludes and diminished arpeggios you've practiced over the last decade or how much of your plucky-ducky self you pour into your instrument. You think it matters that your high school concert band teacher—the one with the overbite and the thinning red hair—said you have *talent*? You really think I care?

Okay. I care. Just a little. Claudette says I use newbie musicians for cannon fodder on the West Village front line, but that's just not true. I like some of you. I favor the kids who ignore me—the ones who tune me out when I'm trying my best to torture them. Sort of like what you're doing right now.

Step lively. Move along. Have a nice day. Hear me? That's a smile in my voice.

You've shown up on loaded shores, my friend. You've scaled Manhattan's sloped shoulders like it's some kind of artisan Everest.

Gotta get to the top, you say. The top of what? In music, there's a very big bottom, but, believe me, there's no top. There's only an endless climb, most of it through mediocrity. Sorry, but that's the truth. Without even thinking to pack a bag lunch or a warm jacket, you keep trudging—lugging your horn, your violin, your trap case, your keyboard, your mallets and reeds and sticks and picks, your books of notes, your desire for brilliance. Don't forget, little guy, you're just one more performer, buoyant and determined to sparkle in the greenish glow of the big city spotlight. Maybe I'll let you glimmer, just for a second, but I'm personal friends with the guy in charge of lighting, and believe me, he's stingy. Besides, Manhattan already gleams enough to make the night sky sickly pale. Your music is the tiniest spark on a neon horizon. You're real, I'm not, but real will only get you so far in this town. It sure as hell won't get you past Claudette's golden door.

What's this? You're giving me the cold shoulder already, and you've only been here a few hours? That's a little rude, don't you think? Look. I could tell you to turn around and go home, but I doubt you'll listen to me. Your own mother warned you not come here and you flipped her the bird. Your college roommate thought you were nuts. Hell, even your great Aunt Edna from Salt Lake City told you I was a mean old bastard, that you'd slip through the fissures, slide into a sinkhole, and end up smoking crack on Avenue A or attending craft classes at Bellevue. Aunt Edna was right. I'm going to give you a nasty-ass hard time—it's my job. Maybe you'll put up with me, maybe not. That's your decision.

I might live in your head, but I'm not entirely heartless. I get it. You want to play. You love your music, the way I once loved mine. But you've got to get a job first. Then you've got to get *to* the job. And then, when that job is over, you have to get another job. Anyone teach you *that* in music school?

You're walking in circles in a city made of squares. I throw you off balance with repeat signs to nowhere, endless vamps, codas that lead you back to where you started. Your music sounds reedy and insipid next to the fat roar of the city's underbelly and the epic rumble of its upper respiratory system. Manhattan sneezes, you're in deep shit. Still, you think what you're doing is beautiful, special even, that you have something to offer the world, that you deserve to be heard.

What the fuck is wrong with you? *Who cares about your music?* I shout again and again. Do you hear me? Nope.

Look out! See? I care. I didn't want you to get hit by that UPS truck. Close call.

I'm trying to be honest with you. It's for your own good. Really, why let a simple melody drag you by your thumbs over rusty grates, when the city will tackle you from behind, throw you out of bounds, and spin you around so many times you won't know Carnegie Hall from Grant's Tomb?

Right. I know the answer. Because you have to be here. You have no choice. That's the thing about Manhattan. You're either dreaming about living here or you're actually here. I like you. You have balls. You made the move.

There. Have a knish. You have to eat something. Feel better? You know, these street vendors have big rat problems. You should see where they store their carts at night. A sin. But a meal is a meal. So enjoy it and try not to think about rodent feces.

Speaking of food, Claudette jokes that I eat musicians for my afternoon snack. Right. I *could* swallow you whole if I wanted to.

But even as your legs dangled from my mighty mouth, even as my capped teeth pulverized your ribs, you would go on practicing your Charlie Parker licks, your Gershwin repertoire, your hip-hop nonstop Brecht, Bach, Bono. It would make me feel bad, crushing your life's work. I guess I'm a softy. I would probably just spit you out and give you another chance.

"Music is my life," you say.

Really, you people are relentless.

I'm your life now. You've invaded my territory, so put on your ratty black outfit, shut up, and pay attention. I know the heroic counterpoint in your practice studio might be louder than my grumbling advice, but leave your ambition on the hot plate, kid, and just this once, listen to me.

You think you can handle anything I hurl in your direction. But once you've used up your inheritance from Grandma Podolinski—which will happen in about three months—finding a way to pay your rent will become more important than any stupid sonata you're trying to master. Survival will be your new art form. You'll sleep on a leaky air mattress in the front hallway of an apartment you share with four other musician wannabes and one pole dancer. You'll eat thirty-nine-cent packages of shrimp-flavored ramen noodles for dinner and bruised pears for breakfast. I can't stand watching this, so I'll cough up a halfway decent music job and toss it like a lukewarm potato into your grateful hands. You'll feel alive and purposeful. You're breaking through. You'll email your parents and boast about the gig, the moldy-fig bandleader, the cute baritone player, the overdressed audience, the catering at the hall. "They gave me food," you'll say, as if a hot meal means a reversal of fortune, a sign that your career is finally on track. Oddly, you'll never mention the music you played.

You'll spend half of what you make that night in a bar on Eighth Avenue, hanging out with a cabaret singer who might be a guy, might be a girl, you're not sure. Do you invite me for a martini? No. It pisses me off. Back to the air mattress for you, Bubble Face. You'll sleep with the pole dancer. Maybe you'll splurge on some onion-garlic bagels for breakfast. Then you'll start practicing again.

It'll be a few years before I lob a steady gig in your direction. You haven't earned that privilege yet. Sorry. There's a waiting list.

Not that I'm trying to discourage you or anything. Believe me, I've given this speech about a million times in the last few decades. I'm trying to get the Port Authority to put my Helpful Words of Advice for Performing Artists on an audio loop at the airports and bus terminals, but the speakers keep busting. Plus, you know, in spite of my good looks, I have an awful voice. I sound a little like Elmer Fudd on helium—too much gin, too many cigars, too many hours patrolling the symphony halls, jazz joints, and rock clubs.

Here's a fun fact: Most of you will give up in less than ten years. Can't say I blame you. Get out while you can. Don't come back. Go somewhere nice. A place with roads instead of avenues. Where you're wanted. Here, you're nothing. A big, fat, artistic nothing. There are better places to be artistic and fat. And there are surely better places to be nothing. But remember, once Manhattan lets you go, the gate slams shut forever. Stand clear of the closing doors.

Pack your precious instrument between your legs and head back to Providence, to Portland, to Pittsburgh, where, I'm told, they actually have roads that go places. Maybe you'll teach. Maybe you'll drink too much. Maybe you'll put down the horn and pick up a baby. Or two. Good luck with that. You'll hate me because I wore you down. But you won't admit it. You'll tell everyone how much you *adored* me—how the years you spent with me were the best. That you had the time of your life.

Eventually, you'll think of me as an old friend, your well-meaning Uncle Manny who taught you a few things about tenacity. Eventually, I'll think of you as one of my own—a tempest-tossed urchin with a song, a kid who tap-danced on my torso, cracked open the golden door, and plucked a few heartstrings along the way. It's only then, decades later, that I'll tell you the truth: You played in tune. You had steady time. You sounded pretty good. I don't really believe in talent, but kid, you had something going on. Not enough, but something. You shouldn't have left.

No need for guilt. No one, and I mean no one, will care that you're gone. Why should they, when another *you* shows up every ten seconds? It's not like you're special or anything. But here's a secret: I'll remember you. I will. Musicians keep my legend alive. Without music Manhattan is just another lump of rock, but don't tell anyone I said that. Especially Claudette.

After you've deserted me and ditched your big-city dreams, you'll figure out how to live with yourself. You'll make up stories. You'll brag about how you conquered me. You'll encourage others to come. The cycle goes on and on. See? I can't lose.

Anyone got an aspirin? That marimba player up in Morningside Heights is driving me nuts. That gal can really play.

I need you. I do. There, I said it. Look, it's worth noting—a few of you will be good enough, tough enough to stay. You will work as musicians and find families here. You will play and laugh and cry and complain. You will talk about leaving, but you won't. You will die on this island, but before you do, you will call it your home. I'll be at your memorial service to pay my respects.

Yes, there will be music.

Sisterhood of Soul

Random puffs of chilly October wind sweep me across town to White's Rehearsal Studio on West Forty-fourth Street. Big day for me—my first gig in Manhattan. I'm prepared to spend the morning playing hard and getting to know the musical strengths and quirks of the women I'll work with for the length of my contract—eighteen months, assuming nothing goes wrong. Management could decide to fire us all. Or they might just hate me. I'm trying to act cool, but I have to admit I'm really psyched. Someone is paying me to play the drums! And I love the idea of playing with female musicians. Since I've spent the last three years playing with a bunch of guys, I'm looking forward to the new vibe. I guess it'll be a lot different, a lot the same.

The sky looks like cream of mushroom soup. Reminds me of home. Pittsburgh. As the wind creeps under the hem of my jacket, I heave my cymbal bag onto my left shoulder and walk as fast as I can, looping my way around clusters of strange-looking people. Maybe it's always this way, but today Manhattan seems like an especially scary carnival ride—complete with surprise plumes of smoke, sirens, bells, and pop-up spooky people who jump out of nowhere. A hotdog vendor makes kiss-kiss noises at me and says, "Hey Mami, Mami, Mami!" as I walk by. I check my watch. I have five minutes to cover this last endless block. God, these cymbals weigh two tons.

As I hustle past the Port Authority Bus Terminal, I pretend to ignore old-looking young women rummaging though garbage cans for scraps of food. I try to distract myself, but no luck. I keep walking, but my eyes refuse to focus on the sidewalk in front of me. My gloom threatens to ruin my day, my week, my life, but then I reach the studio and a door slides open. Nothing like an automatic door to shift a mood from bad to good. I coast through, a little surprised by my nervousness.

"Hi," I say to the security guard. "I'm Jane Bowman. I'm here for an SOS rehearsal? Sisterhood of Soul?"

"Yeah, toots. Take the elevator to the third floor. Sign in here."

The elevator smells like stale cologne and french fries. On the third floor I'm met by a cigar-chomping bald guy in a light-blue blazer.

"You're Jane, right? Drummer? I recognize you from your picture. Thank God you look better in real life. That picture sucks."

"Gee, thanks, and yes, I'm Jane Bowman. How do you do?" I say, extending my hand with Penn Academy politeness.

"Go talk to Mandy Fantalo over in the corner. She'll measure you for your costume. You get to say if you want pink or purple."

"Excuse me?"

"Your dress. Pink or purple. You pick. I don't know crap about this kinda thing. Talk to Mandy."

"Isn't this a rehearsal?" I ask, waving away the cigar smoke.

"Yeah darlin', it's a rehearsal. But the costume shit comes first. We can't do the photos till we have the costumes, and the costumes will take a week or two to make, so we gotta do that first. Got it?"

"I didn't get your name," I say, swallowing the urge to kick him in the shins and run.

"Yeah, yeah, yeah, I'm Bernie Brown," he says, not even looking at me.

"So you're the band manager?" I say.

"Yeah darlin', I'm the manager."

"Let's try this again. How do you do, Mr. Brown," I say, extending my hand once again and holding it there for what seems like ten minutes. Finally he shakes my hand.

"Yeah, yeah, yeah, whatever," he says.

"Very pleased to meet you," I say.

"Yeah, yeah, me too," he says, looking down at his clipboard. "Now could you please get your butt over to Mandy? We got business to do here; this ain't no bingo hall."

"Yes, of course," I say, wondering what a bingo hall looks like. "Pink or purple, right?"

"That's right, darlin'. Pink or purple."

∽

"Hi," says one of the musicians standing in line at Mandy's desk. "I'm Liz." She is short and curvy, with a big tangle of auburn curls trailing down her back. Her voice sounds like a bassoon.

"Hi," I say. "Jane Bowman. Looks like we've been hired for a fashion show instead of a soul band."

"Looks like."

"Pink or purple?" I say, and we burst into laughter. "You're an alto player, right?"

"Right," she says.

"Are we actually going to play today, do you think?"

"I hope so," says Liz. "But it looks like we'll cover a lot of the more important production details first—like costuming. I wonder what would happen if we all picked the same color. It would screw up everything."

"Okie-dokie, next gwoup, come with me!" says a middle-aged bottle blond with straight pins in the corner of her mouth and a measuring tape draped around her neck. "I'm Mandy Fantalo and I'll be doing your costumes!" Mandy leads us into an area draped for privacy.

"Take off your sweaters and dwop your jeans. I gotta get accuwate measurements for these dwesses cause they're supposed to be weally, weally tight. Form fitting. Weally form fitting. Like you can't bend over."

Liz sighs and pulls off the backpack holding her sax. She yanks her sweater over her head.

"Isn't this sort of weird?" I say to her. "I mean, we've been here for five minutes and now we're supposed to take off our clothes?"

"This your first girl-band gig?" she asks.

"Yeah," I say. "I've been playing in a boy band for the last three years. Testosterone central. Pink or purple was not an option."

"All guys? Lucky you. Listen, these girl-band managers are obsessed with costuming. Part of the gimmick, you know. But don't worry, everything is cool here. I worked with Mandy on another gig, and she's a little hyper but basically okay. Kinda heavy-handed with the sequins and hot glue gun if you ask me, but I can live with that. I sorta like the glamour-girl look."

Mandy wraps her measuring tape around Liz's chest.

"Thirty-seven and a half inches," Mandy says to Liz. "You lose weight, hon?"

"Uh, you shouldn't say that until you check the bottom half," says Liz.

"Oh, yeah, I see what you mean. Forty. You gain weight, hon?"

"Just shifting it around a little. I've been temping. You know, desk job."

"Okie-dokie, hon, you're finished," says Mandy. "Pink or purple?"

"Pink."

"What do you do there?" I ask.

"On a temp job? Answer phones mostly."

Another musician, a trumpet player named Patti, says, "You oughta try working with me on your down time."

"Yeah? What are you doin'?" asks Liz.

"Topless car wash."

"You shittin' me?"

"No. It's completely easy, as long as you don't mind being topless and schlepping a long hose."

Isn't it cold? I want to ask, but it seems like a stupid question.

"Isn't it cold?" asks Liz.

"Nah, it's inside. Plus at fifty bucks an hour you learn to live with it if it gets a little nippy. Good for the Nortons, you know. Makes 'em stand up nice and proud."

"Fuck," says Liz.

"So what happens? Do the guys look at you while you wash the car?"

"Yeah. I mean I guess they look. I don't much wanna know what else they're doing in the car while they're checking me out. But I found out if you rub soapsuds all over yourself and squish your chest up against the windshield you can make good tip money. Tits for tips. Or is it tips for tits?"

"Fuck," says Liz.

"Yeah, well I could probably do that, too, but I gotta draw the line somewhere."

Another girl, a stocky electric-bass player from Montana named Betty Wimpner, stands next to me while she waits to be measured.

"Okay, Betty. You're next," says Mandy. "Off with the sweater. Nice wool. Handmade?"

"Yeah, I like to knit in my free time." Betty jerks the sweater over her head. She's not wearing a bra. But that's not what I notice first. She stinks. B.O. Big time. I hope I don't have to sit next to her on the band bus. Holy cow, this is really bad.

"Were you on that Nellie Nigh tour?" Liz asks Betty. "I heard that was a nightmare."

"Yep," says Betty. "Nellie got so drunk she puked onstage one night, all over my amp. I got stories like you wouldn't believe. She's an unbelievable tramp, that woman. Can't keep her hot-pants on. You know, she hired this Brazilian guitar player, Luisa what's-her-name? We called her Lulu. Well, Lulu is like five feet tall and weighs about 70 pounds. Looks like a South American Tinker Bell. Plays the shit out of the guitar, though. Anyway, Nellie taught Lulu how to lap dance, see? One day, on the bus, Nellie started passing Lulu around to all the musicians. We were handing her over our heads from one row to the next."

"Awful," says Liz, laughing.

"That was the band bus entertainment for a while, lap dancing with little Lulu."

This story has temporarily taken my mind off the B.O. Are we ever going to play music?

"Better than those guys on the Buddy Wich tour," says Mandy, with straight pins between her lips. "I heard they got so bored they started whipping each other in the back of the bus, just to see how long they could stand the pain. Widiculous. They had weally big welts and everything."

"No shit?" says Liz.

"So wait," says Betty. "The Nellie Nigh story gets worse. Last winter we were in Montana and Nellie tried to get it on with the lady bus driver. That poor broad was driving through a damn blizzard, and Nellie ripped her bra off and stuffed her face in the lady's tits."

"No shit."

"Wait a minute, did she rip off her own bra or the bus driver's bra?"

"Like it matters. Jesus."

"Really. The worst part was, I think the driver liked it—I mean, it's not like she was yellin' for help. We were swerving all over the road. If it weren't for Carla Sampson grabbing the steering wheel we'd probably all be dead."

"Carla? She's that singer who did backup for Lionel Richie, right? The one with the glass eye?"

"Yeah, that's Carla. Imagine that. A half-blind singer who can drive a bus. Anyway, Nellie had a nervous breakdown ninety days into the tour and had to cancel three months worth of gigs."

"Any cancellation money?"

"I'm not countin' on it, knowin' Nellie. Maybe I should look into the car wash."

Compared to these girls, the boy band back in Pittsburgh seems like a church choir.

"Arms up, hon," says Mandy to Betty.

I don't understand how a person can smell this terrible. I hold my breath. My eyes are starting to cross.

"Oh dear, hon. We have a pwoblem," says Mandy.

I'll say.

"These dwesses are stwapless," she continues. "You're gonna have to shave those pits."

"No way, Mandy," says Betty. "I've never shaved and I'm not gonna start now. My body is my temple."

"That's the hairiest temple I've ever seen," says Patti.

Liz doubles over laughing.

"Okie-dokie, hon, let's see what we've got here," she says to me. By this point I'm not feeling self-conscious, so I unzip my leather jacket and take off my T-shirt. I'm wearing a sports bra, what I always wear when I play. It prevents excess jiggle.

"You've got yourself all smashed down there, hon," she says. "You got a nice figure, why do you want to hide it?"

"I'm not trying to hide anything; it's just that I play better in this bra," I say.

"Okie-dokie, hon, we'll build a nice push-up bwa into your dwess for the show."

"That's going to be a problem, Mandy. I can't play in a dwess. I mean *dress*."

"Yes you can."

"No I can't."

"YES YOU CAN."

"No I won't."

"BERNIE! Get your ass back here."

Bernie, with fear in his eyes, pokes his head around the corner. I can hardly blame him for being nervous. Look at us—a gaggle of girl musicians with dropped drawers and an assortment of motley-looking bras. Plus it smells like French toe cheese in here.

"The little dwummer girl won't wear a stwapless dwess, and it's going to destwoy my costume plot," says Mandy.

"Excuse me," I say. "The little drummer girl will not wear any kind of dress, strapless or not. *Okie-dokie?* I'm a drummer. I play in pants, like every other drummer. Otherwise I don't play. Fire me if you want to."

"Fuck," says Liz.

"She has a contwact," says Mandy. "She's gotta pway."

"You have a contract," growls Bernie. "You've gotta play."

"Yeah, and it says nothing about costumes, or believe me I wouldn't have signed it."

"You know what?" says Betty. "She's right. I'm sick of having to dress up like Barbie just cause I'm a female musician. We might as well work at the car wash with Patti. Tits for tips."

"Jesus," says Bernie.

"This is widiculous," yells Mandy. "Outwageous!"

"Fuck," says Liz.

The discussion travels in circles for several minutes. Eventually the other band members join us and we all threaten to quit if we have to wear costumes that make us look like Cher impersonators. Mandy stomps out of the dressing room in a huff.

"Purple," yells Patti. "I'll take purple!"

"You've got balls, girl," Liz says to me. "Way to go. This may be the first gig I've had where I'll get to look like a normal person."

"Get dressed, all of you," yells Bernie, grinding his cigar between his teeth. "We'll meet on the fifth floor to pass out the charts and start playing through the music."

About time, I think.

"And someone open a window," says Bernie. "It smells like a men's locker room in here."

Black Keys

One morning, in the dawnish glow of a grayish day, she takes her pet rabbits to the vet's office and has them put to sleep. Just like that.

"Maybe I just don't want to take care of them anymore," she whispers to herself. "Maybe I don't. Maybe I don't care. And why should I?" She returns home, picks some roses, puts a carton of milk in the microwave oven and turns it on, and strikes Stanley's Steinway with an old baseball bat. The noise awakens him.

He screams and yells until she cries. He retrieves the milk carton, cleans up the microwave mess, calls the piano technician, and tears apart the bunny hutch, stacking the planks in an overly neat pile by the back door.

Eventually, she stops combing her hair, so he does it for her, untangling the matted clumps tenderly at first, then—when flashes of anger get the better of him—yanking at knots and watching fragile strands, gold and silver all at once, drift to the carpet like broken threads of glass.

She endures numerous tests and he stays at her side through them all. Together, they hear the doctor's diagnosis, delivered by a nurse in a lavender sweater that's worn at the elbows. Stanley's wife smiles, plucking invisible lint from the tweedy chair in the examining room, listening and nodding, as if the terror deserves careful consideration and a polite response.

Later that night, he explains again what the nurse has said, and she understands, for a moment, what lies ahead. She fears for what she hasn't yet lost, and weeps for what might have been. Then she forgets it all, at least for the moment, and falls into a hollow sleep.

⁓

Ten years later, his name and face long forgotten by her, he sits at her bedside, watching, waiting, and wanting for it to end. Soon, very soon, she'll forget how to breathe, how to swallow, how to awaken. Curling in on herself, she'll approach the one place he imagines she longs for, the silent and safe home she knew before there was a world. Seizing air, sipping light, she'll let go of life and return to nothingness, to darkness, to before. But first, she'll live at least another day.

Not knowing what else to do, he clings to solitude and tries not to reminisce. He leaves the nursing home, dashes home briefly to change into his tuxedo, and drives into Manhattan. He strolls into the Plaza Hotel, sits at a grand piano—where he has worked five nights a week for the past fifteen years—and plays her favorite song.

Carol of the Bells

It's Christmas Eve, again. Carol closes her eyes and inhales the holiday air. This Christmas, Carol has stuffed her own stocking with a lot of junk she doesn't want and doesn't need, but the Good Lord told her to buy an Armani lipstick and a Cartier diamond tennis bracelet and so she did. She closes her eyes and thanks God for her warm and beautifully decorated home. God is good; God is great; God looks out for her. Husband or not, she will sing and play her way into seasonal rapture. O come all ye faithful.

Carol thinks back to a year ago. She hadn't meant to kill her husband, Dick, especially not on Christmas Eve and certainly not by shoving him down the rickety wooden steps leading to the church's back door.

Carol looks in the mirror, brushes her baby-fine hair, applies her new lipstick, and tries not to fret. Tonight she will sing a big solo at the annual candlelight service and Nativity scene. Then she will think about her future. Maybe she'll sell the house and head back to New York City, maybe even give her opera career another try. God will tell her what to do. God, she has discovered, always has a plan.

Twelve months ago Dick Davis was stumbling around the living room, his handsome but bloated face flushed and rutted by the contents of a bottle of Glenlivet. He guzzled it while Carol prepared to leave for her Christmas Eve performance at the church.

"Come on, honey, one last drink before you ring the chimes for the Bible thumpers," he said.

"I don't want a drink. And they are not chimes," Carol replied. "They are handbells. And the members of the bell choir are decent, God-fearing citizens. And may I remind you, Dick, that we won the handbell regionals this year. We are champions. And furthermore, the members of the choir are not Bible thumpers. They are our neighbors."

"Yeah, yeah, yeah. Carol Davis and the Ding Dongs. Ding-a-ling. Ding-dong-ding."

"Please, Dick."

"Could ya get me another drink, hon? And maybe you could take off your top while you're at it? Your church lady routine turns me on."

Sometimes when he got like this, she would strip down to her skirt just to get him to shut up. She knew when he was too drunk to do more than stare.

༄

This year will be different. Dick is dead. Carol rinses out her teacup, touches the ruby-encrusted gold cross hanging around her neck, buttons the top loop of her best white cotton blouse—the one with puffy sleeves and a collar that lies flat under her blue velvet choir robe—and blows out a "Home for the Holidays" vanilla-almond-musk candle sitting on the kitchen windowsill. A curly line of smoke rises from the wick. Just about anything smells better than scotch.

Carol arranges back issues of *O* and *Good Housekeeping* magazines on her coffee table—she prefers them to fan out diagonally—and heads to the foyer. She wraps herself in her favorite coat and pulls on her Uggs. Despite the layers of cashmere, suede, and fur she feels as transparent as a tissue-paper page in a church hymnal. She adds another scarf. There. She locks the door of her Georgian-style house and begins the long walk down the hill to the little white church in the valley. The slope is neither slippery nor steep, but the pitch of the road causes Carol to lean backward as she walks forward, like a mime strolling in place. There's a dusting, a puff, a glove of snow on the road and, even from this high up, Carol can spot the radiant path leading to Haven Heights Crossroads. Every year on Christmas Eve residents fill paper bags with coarse sand and lighted candles—outlining the town with a one-night-only luminous walkway that lures the faithful right to the front door of the church.

Ten years. For ten years she has lived here. Now, a widow at thirty-two, not very happy and not very sad, she organizes thoughts the way she organizes music. One note at a time. With God's help, she'll know how her song is supposed to end. In the meantime she walks toward the church, greeting neighbors as she goes.

"Good evening, Mr. Ramsel. Merry Christmas to you!"

"Evening, Mizz Davis. Expect this will be a difficult holiday for you, Ma'am." He pauses and looks down at the snow. "To think it was exactly one year ago tonight. My heart goes out to you. I know you're still grieving."

"Oh, I'll be fine, Mr. Ramsel. The Lord takes care of me."

"I suppose he does. But I'm praying for you, Ma'am."

"Thank you very much. I can use all the help I can get."

"Can't we all? Will the Clappers be playing 'The Little Drummer Boy' this year? Always one of my favorites—and it sounds just right on those bells. *Pa rumpa-pum-pum.*"

"Yes, sir. All the old favorites. The classics. The songs God wants us to sing."

"Good. Maybe we're old-fashioned in these parts, but we don't take kindly to those modern Christmas songs. I hope you're planning to stay in Crossroads, Mizz Davis. The church needs you. And, you know, we take care of our widows in this town. We protect them, if you know what I mean."

"I hear you, Mr. Ramsel. Tell your lovely wife I hope she's feeling better. God bless both of you."

&

The songs God wants us to sing. A decade ago Carol had been a confident graduate of the Eastman School of Music, a coloratura soprano with a promising career and no interest at all in church music. On her professors' advice, she moved to Manhattan and continued the rigorous process of stretching and coaxing her voice to meet the demands of an opera career. After a year she was ready for major challenges. But then, one month before her scheduled audition at the Met, she met and fell in love with Dick Davis. Dashing Dick— that's what she called him—had just received his PhD in structural engineering from Columbia. When Carol failed to get a callback at the Met, she decided to abandon her dreams of vocal stardom and focus on her man. Dick proposed, Carol gave up the career she never had, and the two of them moved to West Virginia, where

Dick accepted a corporate job supervising the repair of structural deficiencies in coal mines. Carol and Dick built a villa on a big hill, looking down on the tiny homes of churchgoing miners and their ever-growing families.

Coal rules in Crossroads, West Virginia. The town, charming and ravaged all at once, doesn't offer many job opportunities for budding opera singers. Carol, crazy in love but looking for a musical outlet, accepted a volunteer position as Minister of Music at the local church. Growing up, she had never taken part in organized religion, nor had she attended services on a regular basis. When she started working at the church she didn't really believe in God, but she did believe in the power of music. "If you've got a good song or two," she used to say to Dick, "you've got your own set of angels."

While Dick conferred and consulted with mine owners and union officials and traveled around the state, Carol planned musical selections for weekly church services, rehearsed and conducted an aging band—an accordion, two banjos and a clarinet—and organized a red-cheeked children's vocal group. When a group of church members asked about starting a handbell choir, Carol bought the bells herself, with Dick's blessing. She hadn't expected to enjoy the bells so much, but they were beautiful—handheld brassy bowls of hope, silent and gleaming, waiting to be caressed and rung. When the choir lifted their bells and began to play, prisms of sound would bounce around the sanctuary. One spring day, when the church windows were open, Dick told her he could hear the bells at home, echoing through the hollow, shaming the birds and chasing away the dusty winter. He said things like that, back then.

For about three years Carol thought her life was perfect. Then the accident happened: The earth crumbled, crashed, and crushed the life out of four of Crossroad's miners. No one in the community blamed Dick—he had been consulting on a project outside of Crossroads at the time—but he blamed himself. Afterward, he stayed sober during the day, but in the evening, as soon as the sun dipped behind the scooped-out hills, he drank, pouring more darkness into himself, as if the black night alone could never be enough.

Carol, confused and alarmed by the change in Dick's personality, turned herself over to God and handbells. She treasured the love and support of the Crossroads congregation. She began to pray with them. She found peace. Carol offered her music to God, and God listened. He even approved.

Dick drank Scotch; Carol embraced Jesus.

༄

As Carol approaches the church this evening she runs right into Mrs. Zweiffler and her seven children, all of them wearing matching hats knitted by a weary mother with nervous hands. Two of the older children, seventeen-year-old twin boys named Nat and Noel, ring bells with the Crossroads Clappers. Their father died three years ago of lung disease.

"Looking forward to this evening, Mrs. Zweiffler?" asks Carol.

"Best night of the year," says Mrs. Zweiffler as she wipes the nose of her six-year-old. "For God's sake, young man, blow your nose—don't just stand there."

"Noel is nervous about his solo on 'We Three Kings,'" says Nat. "If you want I can play it for him."

"I'm sure Noel will do just fine," says Carol. "Now get inside before your hands freeze. Can't have my star ringers with frostbitten fingers. I'll be in shortly. And remember to tell everyone to—"

"Be prepared!" say Nat and Noel in unison. In another ten months they'll both be working in the mines. This will be their last Christmas Eve performance with Carol. Next year at this time they'll be exhausted young men, part of the congregation, pretending to be grown up while quietly singing Christmas hymns Carol taught them. Their hair will be damp and slicked back, and, like the other adult men, they will pick at the dirt underneath fingernails they thought they had scrubbed clean.

"Merry Christmas, Mizz Davis," says Mrs. Zweiffler. "I hear you'll be singing a solo this evening. We can hardly wait—it'll be like having a real live angel in the sanctuary with us."

"I'll do my best," says Carol. "I'll try and make the angels proud."

"You come sit with us in the Fellowship Hall after the service. I know what it's like to be without a husband on Christmas Eve. We'll take care of you. As long as you're in Crossroads, we'll make sure you're safe."

"Thank you, Mrs. Zweiffler. I'll be happy to join you."

"I made snickerdoodles!"

"All the more reason to celebrate."

༄

Carol watches for a moment as the Zweifflers file into Haven Heights Crossroads. There's a crossroads at Haven Heights, for sure, but it's a vertical intersection. Either you head down into the mines or let yourself be lifted into the arms of Jesus. Not much of a choice, really—a miner's light or a crown of thorns. Everything else becomes a necessary distraction from the other two options. Carol's music bridges the space between down there and up high—a middle place where untarnished clouds shelter rocky ground. On nights like this, Carol knows she has been sent here to do God's work.

"It's not just the miners descending into that pit every day," says Reverend Clem Salisbury. "The rest of us go with them—the wives, the children, the mothers and grandparents, those of us who love and care about these hard-working Christians. Every one of us steps on that elevator at dawn and plunges into the darkness. It's here, in this church, where we retrieve the light."

Carol stops by the back door to the church and sits on a small bench with a plaque that says GOD BLESS OUR FALLEN MINERS. She runs her fingers over the polished brass. The plaque feels cold in the center and sharp around the edges, like broken ice.

At this time last year, Carol convinced herself that if Dick showed up at the Christmas Eve service he would hear the glorious sound of the bell choir, sober up, respect her work, respect the church, and find a little comfort and joy in the midnight candlelight ritual. She would never get him to believe in God, but maybe he could believe in the bells. That would be enough. Too drunk to argue, Dick agreed to tag along.

While singing a rousing arrangement of "Joy to the World," Carol and the Crossroads Clappers marched into the sanctuary, followed by the children's choir, several wheezing ushers, and the lucky church members chosen to take part in this year's Nativity scene. Carol spotted Dick slumped in a back pew, not exactly sleeping, but not quite awake. She smiled and waved, happy to see him there.

The service started. The congregation prayed and sang and listened to Scripture. When the time came for the bell choir feature, Carol turned to cue Mrs. Miscamarra, the organist. From the corner of her eye she saw Dick sit up straight. *Good*, she thought, *he's paying attention.*

Carol shifted her focus to the task at hand—making sure Mrs. Miscamarra had the tempo right, that all of the white-gloved Clappers were ready to ring, that the woman playing Mary was in place and ready to place Baby Jesus—swaddling clothes and all—in the manger, that Mrs. Mitchell was alert and ready to ring the all-important pickup note to "What Child Is This?"

The Crossroads Clappers took pride in their precision, with each white-gloved member responsible for at least two tones in every song. Carol's arrangement of "What Child Is This?" was in D minor. But Orville Rudolph, in charge of the "A" bell—a critical tone in D minor—had disobeyed Carol's first rule of bell choir etiquette: Poor old Orville, a hulking guy with a chapped ego and a Christmas-y name, had neglected to make sure his bells' strike points were in the proper position. Had he done so, he would have surely noticed the missing clapper. The "A" clapper was gone—removed by a mean-spirited ringer or maybe even by Mrs. Rudolph, who thought Orville had a crush on Carol. When Orville raised his bell to ring it, there was nothing, not a sound. Silent night. He flipped his bell upside down and peered into it, as if the clapper would magically grow back if he stared long enough.

That's when Dick Davis laughed. Loudly. He might have been in a back pew, but everyone in the church could hear him.

A confused Mary held a squirming Baby Jesus, Orville Rudolph searched for his clapper, and Mrs. Miscamarra—whose shaky sense of rhythm collapsed when she couldn't hear Orville's missing bell tone—panicked and began playing in double time, turning the lilting ballad into a polka.

Carol continued conducting, but Orville, once he recovered from his shock, reached across Betty Lou Stutz, snatched one of her bells, and began ringing—the wrong tone—in a frenzied attempt to fill the silence. Bad enough, but Betty Lou, incensed that Orville had swiped her bell, reached back across the table to retrieve it, and, with one velvet-sleeved arm, swept two bells, a couple of mallets, and a hand chime to the granite floor.

Oh, the noise. The music stammered to a halt and a thick silence swallowed the church.

That's when Carol heard Dick's booming voice: "Take your top off, Carol! Show us your tits!" Then he laughed. And laughed. And laughed. Gradually, the congregation joined him—an uncomfortable laugh, like the sound of squeaking elves or computerized toys with low batteries.

Baby Jesus wailed, Mary tripped over the swaddling clothes, one of the goats (dressed as a sheep) peed on the stage, and Reverend Clem jumped to the pulpit and suggested they skip the Nativity scene and get on with the candle-lighting ceremony and cookie exchange.

The Crossroads Clappers, mortified by Orville's conduct and alarmed by Dick Davis's guffaws—he screeched in unison with Baby Jesus's squeals—skulked back to the choir loft.

Carol raced from the sanctuary and into the upstairs Fellowship Hall and sobbed, her face prickling with shame. She stormed back and forth in the empty room, ripped off her choir robe, threw it on the floor, and stomped on it.

Dick left the church through the front door and circled around to the back. He climbed the tall stairs leading to the Fellowship

Hall. Out of breath and dizzy from the adrenaline rush, he yanked open the door and balanced on the top step. "Come on, Carol," he yelled. "Ring those chimes."

Carol raced across the polished linoleum floor of the hall—the room meant for potluck dinners, pancake breakfasts, and ice-cream socials; the very place where Carol had attended the funeral lunch held for the four miners killed seven years ago; the space where residents of Crossroads met to compare notes on child-raising and herbal remedies for respiratory disease; the empty hall that had hosted hundreds of hours of bell choir rehearsal; the room of a thousand wrong notes and even more right ones.

Carol flew to face her husband, her perfect white blouse flapping like a misshapen angel wing. When she reached the doorway, she hovered for a moment and waited for God to tell her what to do. Silence. She opened her arms and reached for Dick. When he reached back, as if to embrace her, Carol shoved Dick Davis down the flight of stairs.

Before Dick even hit the bottom, Carol swirled around and picked up her filthy choir robe. She brushed it off, folded it into a neat rectangle, and placed it on a cookie table. After retrieving her coat and boots from the cloak corner, she left the hall.

At the bottom of the staircase, Carol stepped over Dick's crumpled body. He had landed on his knees, with his head in his hands. He almost looked like he was praying. She nudged him with her foot. Dead. She sighed, adjusted her scarf, pulled on her hat, and headed back up the hill, toward home.

An hour later, Carol sat in front of her fireplace with a cup of chamomile tea. She thumbed through the December issue of *Good Housekeeping*. Mr. and Mrs. Ramsel arrived to give her the news.

"There's been a terrible *accident*," said Mr. Ramsel.

"Terrible," said Mrs. Ramsel. "Just terrible."

"It's Mr. Davis. Looks like he fell down the steps. Terrible accident."

"Everyone says it's a terrible tragedy," said Mrs. Ramsel. "And an *accident*."

"Yes, terrible." said Mr. Ramsel. "I *saw* him slip and fall. It was terrible. Must have been the alcohol."

"Must have been," said Mrs. Ramsel. "Terrible. May God look after his poor soul. May he rest in peace."

"Mrs. Zweiffler sent snickerdoodles," said Mrs. Ramsel as she uncovered a paper plate of cookies. "We spoke to the police. We told them what we saw. We told them he slipped on those old steps. We told them, yes we did. We told them good. They've taken Mr. Davis's body to the morgue in Sistersville. We know you must be suffering from the terrible shock."

"The shock. The terrible shock."

"Anything we can do for you?"

"No, thank you," Carol said, arranging a lace doily on her dining table. "Nothing at all. God always has a plan. Would you like some eggnog?"

༄

Tonight, thinks Carol, *will be different*. The children will sing, the bells will ring, and Baby Jesus's swaddling clothes will keep him warm and snug in the manger. Mrs. Miscamarra will not turn the time around, the goat disguised as a sheep will not pee, Orville Rudolph will check his clappers before the service, Mrs. Stutz will not fling her brass bells onto the stone floor, and Dick Davis will not laugh at her. Tonight Carol Davis will step forward and sing a solo, a showy interpretation of "O Holy Night" accompanied by the Crossroads Clappers. Carol has found her audience and she has found her voice. The sanctuary will overflow with sounds of sorrow and joy, of passion and indifference—an acoustic version of coarse sand and light. God will look down on her and smile. Nothing will get in her way. Nothing.

Carols stands, touches the ruby cross hanging around her neck, glances back at the path of candles in paper bags, brushes invisible wrinkles from her coat, looks down at the frosted earth, peers at the fragile sky, and begins to sing her warm-up scales. She makes a decision: She'll stay in Crossroads, at least for another year. The church needs her music. And she needs their protection. A mutually beneficial deal, all arranged by the grace of God. She belongs here.

Pink

At least the water is hot. Kim stands on her toes in the musty pink-tiled shower, rinses her hair one last time, and tries not to touch anything. She hates this bathroom. Even though she has scrubbed it a hundred times, it still feels moldy. With one finger, she slides back the pink plastic shower curtain and grabs a thin pink towel from the rack next to the shower stall. She has sublet this rooftop Long Island City apartment—spacious by New York City standards—from a guy named Eddie Small. Kim has never met Mr. Small in person, but Mr. Lopez, the Peruvian building superintendent, says Eddie Small has a lot of respect for color. Eddie calls his apartment a Study in Raspberry.

Skittle, scrape, scritch-scratch.

God, what's that noise? For weeks Kim has been hearing something in the bathroom, right over the medicine cabinet. She looks up at the pink acoustic tiles lining the ceiling, but there's nothing to see. Just more pink. Kim has told Mr. Lopez about the noise, but he shrugs, throws his hands in the air, and says, "Keem"—he calls her Keem—"It's New York Ceety. There are many things we no can esplain."

Kim rakes a comb through her short hair and looks in the mirror over the sink. Not bad. Dark beige skin, big bones, defined muscles, long limbs. Strong. Fierce. She is twenty-three years old, a marathon runner, a talented but inexperienced baritone saxophone player, and a recent graduate of the Berklee College of Music. Good thing Kim keeps in shape—the baritone is over three feet long and weighs about fourteen pounds.

After two months of living as an unemployed jazz musician she has finally—finally!—gotten her first New York City gig—a three-hour club date at the Metropolitan Museum, playing with an all-female big band called Jamie Johnston's Jazz Kittens. The musician who usually plays baritone fell off a riser last week and broke her arm. Jamie called Kim to sub.

Scritch-scratch.

Kim ignores the noise and slathers on sesame body oil. She has spent the past few months practicing, playing jam sessions, running, practicing some more, networking with musicians and contractors, and listening over and over again to her collection of Mulligan, Miles, and Monk recordings. She has worked hard, determined that this day would come. She smiles at herself in the mirror, poses like a bodybuilder and laughs out loud. Once Jamie Johnston hears her play she'll surely get calls for other gigs. Just in time, too. The money she has been living on, a small inheritance from her grandmother, is running out. She'll need to pay Mr. Lopez another $2,000 in just a few days.

Scritch-scratch. Bunga-bunga. Bam.

What a racket. What's living in the ceiling—a family of four? Kim drowns out the noise with her blow-dryer and thinks about Jamie Johnston. Jamie used to be a man. His name was Jimmy Johnston back then. Now, three years after major surgery and God only knows how many wigs, wardrobe consultations, and hormone treatments, Jimmy has morphed into Jamie, a gorgeous woman with curly red hair, decent-sized breasts, and her very own big band.

As excited as Kim is about the gig—Jamie is a great bandleader—Kim really hates the idea of an all-female band. At Berklee there was never an all-female *anything*. True, female instrumentalists were in the minority, but, still, the band was the band. Kim knows she is lucky to have gotten this gig, but she has mixed feelings about performing with a group called the Jazz Kittens—like she's taking part in a musical circus sideshow. *Step right up folks! Presenting Frieda the Fat Trombonist; Ping and Pong, the Siamese-Twin Violists; Tiny Tom Thumb with his Normal-Sized Organ; the Aborigine Oboe Trio; the Jazz Kittens All-Girl Big Band.*

Stupid.

At least Jamie Johnston *used* to be a man. Kim thinks that counts for something, although she's not exactly sure what. Someday, she swears, she'll have her own damn band. And she'll pick the best musicians to play with her. No gimmicks. Kim refuses to be negative today. She laughs again and flexes her biceps. She flips off the blow-dryer, examines a blemish on her forehead, and picks up her tinted sunscreen.

BAM! BAM! BAM!

Oh, no. Kim looks up just as one of the pink acoustic tiles cracks open. Before she can scream, duck, or even scoot to one side, a huge living thing with sharp claws and oily fur drops onto her head, bounces into and out of the sink, and scampers across the pink linoleum. The size of a small dog, it darts back and forth in the bathroom, snarling and bearing its pointy teeth.

"Fuck, fuck, fuck, fuck, fuck," Kim shouts as she hops back and forth. "Get away from me!" She scoots around the rat-dog, slams the bathroom door behind her, leaps through the pink apartment, and runs into the hallway screaming. She swats at her head, imagining the rat-dog still tangled in her hair. She is naked, but she doesn't care.

"Oh my God, oh my God, oh my God—HELP!"

Mr. Lopez, who lives in the apartment next door, steps into the hallway.

"Keem, Keem," he yells. "Get a greep, Keem. What is wrong? Talk to me, Keem."

Kim, her body slick with sesame oil and spotted with clumps of pink plaster dust, springs into his arms, hyperventilating and wrestling with the rat-dog she still feels on her head. Mr. Lopez puts her down and shakes her.

"Talk to me, Keem. I cannot help unless you talk to me."

"It's on my h-h-head." She gulps air.

"On your head there is nothing. Except maybe some pink paint and sparkling hair gel. Calm down. Please."

Kim takes several deep breaths while Mr. Lopez runs into his own apartment and fetches a blanket.

"Sweet baby Jesus, cover yourself up," he says as he throws the blanket over her. "Now talk to me."

"Mr. L-l-lopez," says Kim between hiccoughs and sobs. "There is something in my bathroom. It crashed through the ceiling. It's b-b-big and f-f-furry and it attacked m-m-me."

"Mother of Jesus," says Mr. Lopez, crossing himself. "It finally happened." He crosses himself again. "You wait here."

Kim clutches the blanket while Mr. Lopez heads back into his apartment. When he returns he is carrying a large wooden baseball bat.

"Oh, please be careful!" says Kim, as she watches Mr. Lopez, his shoulders tense, his back straight, enter her apartment. She peeks through the front door and watches him sneaking into the bathroom, baseball bat over one shoulder.

The door crashes shut behind him. Then Kim hears the worst noise she has ever heard—one long duet of shrieking and thumping, accompanied by Mr. Lopez's Peruvian tirade.

Silence.

When Mr. Lopez returns to the hallway he is sweating. "That thing," he says, "was a beetch to keel."

"What was it? *What?*" says Kim.

"A mega rat."

"A mega rat?"

"A mega rat. Biggest one I've ever seen. But don't worry; be happy. He's dead now. Do you want him?"

"Do I *want* him? NO! Why would I want a dead mega rat?"

"Okay then. Can I have heem?"

"Y-y-yes. Okay. Please just get him out of there."

"You wait here." Again, Mr. Lopez enters his own apartment. This time he returns wearing rubber boots and gloves and carrying a large industrial garbage bag. He goes back to Kim's bathroom. She listens to him grunt as he struggles to stuff the mega rat into the sack.

"You sure?" he says as he drags the heavy bag through the hallway toward his front door. "You don't want heem?"

"Yes," says Kim. "Th-th-thank you, Mr. Lopez."

"Wait until my wife sees this!" he says. He closes his door.

Kim shivers in the hallway, wondering if she will ever be able to set foot in her apartment again, let alone use the bathroom. Then she remembers her gig. Her gig! Her big chance with Jamie Johnston's Jazz Kittens. A different sort of panic sets in. She raps on Mr. Lopez's front door.

"What, Keem? Is there another one?"

"No, sir. I don't think so. But I need your help. I'm, well, I'm afraid to go back into my apartment and I have a gig this afternoon."

"A geeg?"

"Yes. A job. With a band."

"On that saxophone you play? You sound pretty good. You make a powerful sound. You play like a real man."

"Uh, okay. But, uh, I need to get my clothes and my horn and my bag and my phone out of the apartment so I can get there on time. It's my big chance and I can't be late. If I tell you where everything is, maybe you could help me. I can't go back in there. I just can't."

"Oh, Keem. Why you acting like a girl all the sudden? The mega rat is gone. You gonna let one dead mega rat hold you back from your dreams? You stronger than that. Now come on. I stand outside the door and you go back in—the mega rat is in my freezer. He's not goin' anywhere."

"But what if there's another one?" says Kim.

"There's always another mega rat somewhere," says Mr. Lopez. "But he won't be at your place. At least not today. I feex your ceiling tomorrow. Until then, you use my bathroom. Now go on, don't screw up the geeg because a mega rat dropped on your head. Be strong. Go play your music. And wipe that stuff off your face. You're all pink."

Kim takes a deep breath—she is growing dizzy from all the deep breathing—and sprints back into her rosy apartment. She grabs a kitchen towel and removes pink paint flecks from her hair and face. She throws on her tight black dress and her Nikes, puts her high heels in her bag, grabs her keys and her horn in its soft, black padded case. Weighted down and out of breath, she says goodbye to

Mr. Lopez, treks down five flights of steps to street level, and takes the train to Manhattan.

In no time at all, she's entering the Metropolitan Museum, still brushing pink dust from her shoulders.

"Good afternoon," she says to the guard on duty. "I'm a musician. I'm scheduled to play here today."

"Jazz Kitten?" says the guard. "You look like a Jazz Kitten. Except for that horn. Jesus. It's huge. What is it, a tuba?"

"No. It's a baritone sax," says Kim. "My name is—"

"Doesn't matter. Through the Egyptian room, make a left at the Glass Gallery, head to the reflecting pool, make a right. You need any help with that thing?"

"No. I've got it," she says.

"Really?"

"Really. I've got it." Kim picks up her horn, squares her shoulders, and makes her way.

The Grand Handini

"So. Where do I set up?" Paul Lewinsky, also known as The Grand Handini, has arrived at the Turtle Creek Moose Club in Pittsburgh, ready for his Saturday afternoon gig. He scopes out the hall. Acoustics might present a challenge in this place.

"I don't really care where you set up," says Lois, the waitress. A tiny thing, barely five feet tall, she balances a huge platter of goldfish bowls on her hip. She waves towards a small platform at the end of the room. "Maybe over there? On the stage?" Water sloshes onto the floor. "Jesus Christ. Whoever thought of using live goldfish for centerpieces? I feel like I should call PETA or something."

"Are those real fish?" says Handini, peering into one of the bowls. A tangerine-colored creature swims in circles. "Really? Real fish?" Handini has worked his share of classy joints, but this isn't one of them. Low ceilings, linoleum the color of muddy water, no curtains on the crusty windows. Glossy magenta paper plates with matching napkins and plastic forks adorn each of the twenty picnic tables. The room smells tangy and musty at the same time, like leftover olives.

"Yep. Real fish. Plastic plates. Go figure." Lois knows how to handle musicians. She used to play bass in a local metal band, a five-piece ensemble called Turtle Whack. She quit when her second daughter was born. The baby's father, Turtle Whack's lead singer, ran off with the chick drummer, and now Lois pays the bills by waitressing at other people's weddings. She feels sorry for wedding musicians. Not much better than waitressing. "So you need to load in your equipment or what?" she asks Handini. "You play keyboard, right?"

"Uh, no. I'm a manualist."

"Huh?"

"A hand artist."

"A hand artist? What? You paint or something? Onofrio said there was music for today's reception."

"I *am* a musician. I make music with my hands," says Handini. He steps closer to the waitress, clamps his fists together and makes squishy farting noises through the air holes next to his thumbs. "Hear that? 'Alley Cat!'" He plays another eight bars. The waitress stares at him.

"That's totally weird."

"Trust me, people love this stuff."

"Yeah, yeah. Whatevs. What's your name?"

"The Grand Handini. And you?"

"Bad Ass Lois. How do you do?" Lois knocks over a bowl and a goldfish flops onto a magenta napkin. Handini grabs the fish by the tail, tosses him into a pitcher of water, and wipes his hands on his pants.

"Nice to meet you, Bad Ass Lois. Sorry, I can't shake," he says. "Have to protect my instruments."

"Right," says Lois, extracting the fish from the pitcher with a plastic spoon. "I'm just wondering what's gonna happen to these poor fish once the party is over."

Not one to resist a perfectly good cue for a song, Handini plays a few bars of "The Party's Over." Lois ignores him.

"You got an aquarium?" says Handini.

"No. Do you?"

"No. So. What time does the sound man get here?"

"The sound man?"

"Yeah. I need amplification. A microphone. My music is very delicate."

"I gotta call the boss." Lois slips a cell phone out of her apron pocket. "Onofrio! It's me. The Grand Handini is here and he needs a microphone." She hangs up. "So," she says to Handini, "I'm curious. What's your opening number?"

"Usually a waltz. I like Strauss. But this is a Baptist wedding. No dancing. So I think I'll start with 'Pop Goes the Weasel.' Always a big crowd pleaser."

"You're gonna play 'Pop Goes the Weasel' for a wedding reception? With farting noises? On your hands?"

"Trust me, Lois. Works like a million bucks. Oh! One other thing. I'm gonna need a table for my merchandise."

"Your merchandise?"

"Yeah. I sell CDs. My latest recording is *The Grand Handini Plays Mancini*. You know, 'Pink Panther,' 'Moon River,' 'Peter Gunn.' All the Mancini classics. I've also got *Handini does Garth Brooks*, *Handini Meets Handel*, and *Bebop Handini*. They're all pretty good. But two years ago I recorded a nice set of lullabies for kids. That's my most popular CD to date. It has a new-age vibe. I'm very proud of my manual interpretation of Pachelbel Canon in D. Parents tell me they play it at bedtime for their kids and—*bam!*—the little snots are sawing logs in minutes. Hand diazepam. Better than George Winston."

Lois, not sure she believes anything Handini says, folds each napkin into an origami swan. Handini follows her from place setting to place setting. The goldfish, crescents of light in the dingy hall, stare at her from their glass spheres.

"Poor things," says Lois. Handini laughs; Lois glares at him.

"You know, I also got T-shirts and coffee mugs with a full-color picture of my fists. They make great Christmas presents. If you want one, let me know. I offer a special price to my coworkers."

Lois picks up her phone again. "Onofrio, we need a table for The Grand Handini. He sells stuff. What? I dunno. Bebop CDs and coffee cups. Good. See you in fifteen."

"Wow," says Handini, picking up one of Lois's origami swans. "You're a hand artist yourself. Ever consider selling these? You'd make a fortune."

"Look, I got work to do. Don't you have to warm up or something?"

Handini lifts his hands and begins playing the piccolo solo from "The Stars and Stripes Forever." He whizzes through it while Lois looks on.

"Damn," says Lois. "That's really, uh, astonishing. Awesome. Guess you really don't need to warm up."

"Nope. I'm ready to go. That's the beauty of my profession. I've got my instrument ready at all times. I just keep my hands in my pockets for a few minutes before I go on, and—*giddyup!*—it's off to the races with The Grand Handini. Want some help with those swans?"

"Wouldn't want you to get a paper cut."

"Right. Good thinking. One little skin injury and I'm screwed. Back in 1995 I grabbed an envelope the wrong way and it put me out of business for an entire month."

"Yeah," says Lois. "I hear you. Back when I was still playing I—"

"Whoa!" says Handini. "I knew there was something special about you. You're a musician?"

"Was," says Lois.

"Let me guess," says Handini, looking her up and down. "Flute?"

"No."

"Clarinet?"

"No."

"Oboe?"

"What, are you gonna guess all the wimpy instruments just 'cause I'm short? I am—was—a bass player. Electric bass. Bad Ass Lois. I wasn't kidding with the name."

"Ah," says Handini. "The pork chop. Should have known from the tatts and the lip piercing."

"Yep. Metal band. I quit a few years ago. Long story. Now I'm schlepping trays of goldfish through a tacky catering hall."

"Too bad you don't have your ax with you," says Handini. "We could do a couple of duets."

"I haven't played for a long time," says Lois. "Besides, I don't think you'd much like my music. Metal is a long way from Mancini."

"What? I love metal. I recorded a CD of Iron Maiden covers—you should have heard the solo I took on "Wasted Years"—but my manager told me I'd never be able to move it. So I'm sitting on the master, waiting for the right moment. I'm moving to New York City next year. Enough of this small town stuff."

"You're certainly versatile," says Lois, finishing up the last of the napkins and tucking a loose stand of pink hair behind her ear. "You should do well in New York." She smiles at Handini. Nice. Lois usually feels tired and wired and sort of lonely. When she's not at the catering hall, she works part-time for a dry cleaner, trying not to inhale fumes or get her arms tangled in thin plastic bags and wire hangers. She misses music, but her work schedule doesn't leave time for jam sessions and practicing. It's nice to hang with a guy who clearly loves his job.

"You gotta be flexible in this business," says Handini. "You wouldn't believe the requests I get. Just last night I had to play 'Lush Life,' followed by a medley of Cat Stevens tunes. Fun! Hey, do you think I could get something to eat before the show?"

"I dunno," says Lois. "Caterer is in the kitchen. Go back there and see what's up. From the look of this event, we're talking chipped-ham sandwiches and potato salad."

"Wanna join me?" asks Handini. "A professional musician never turns down a free meal, especially if there's a pretty girl attached to it."

Lois hesitates.

"I'll play dinner music for us! I think I still have some Black Sabbath tunes in my hands," he says. "You can teach me the bass line to 'Electric Funeral.'"

"Never liked that one much," says Lois. "How about 'Wicked World?'"

"Sounds good to me," says Handini. "Drat!" He points to a dead fish in the bowl next to him. "We got a floater here."

Lois, distraught, reaches for the fishbowl. Handini grabs her arm, then pulls back and puts his fists together.

"Don't," says Lois. "Don't you dare play anything."

"'Taps?'" says Handini.

"No."

"Something from *Finding Nemo*? 'You'll Never Walk Alone?'"

"Don't." Lois looks at the fish in the neighboring bowl. "Do fish cry?" she asks.

Handini pauses for a moment, puts his hands in his pockets, and says, "Maybe. But not this one. He's a goner."

"The guests will arrive in thirty minutes," says Lois. "Come on."

Handini and Lois retreat to the Turtle Creek Moose Club kitchen, where they eat Isaly's chipped ham on Wonder Bread. Handini protects his hands; Lois frets about the dead goldfish; they talk about music. Together they sip diet colas through plastic straws that bend in the middle.

No Nonsense Fairy

You've had No Nonsense Fairy sitting on your shoulder since you were eight years old. That's when your mother, who was drunk and lurching past the Dior counter in Bloomingdale's, slapped herself on the forehead and said: "Good grief, I totally forgot! Your birthday was last week. Go ahead, honey. Pick out a nice voice for yourself."

"But I'm only eight," you said. "Why do I have to find my voice now? What if I don't like the voice when I grow up? And what if I don't want to be a singer like you? What if I would rather play guitar?"

"What if, what if. No one wants soap in beer," said Mother, "but everyone wants the suds." Mother talked like that, in riddles. You never quite understood what she was trying to say. Still, you laughed along with her. Mother would often fan the air and reach for your hand without actually touching it. Fluent in dramatic gestures accompanied by babble and scat—the native tongue of lounge singers—Mother could be shiny and amusing in a cocktail bar, but murky in real life. Her personality resembled a small storm cloud—it passed over quickly and left you a little windblown and slightly damp. You wanted to catch the cloud and pass it to her on a pretty silver tray. She might not be around much longer; you knew that. You knew that—outside of a smoky lounge—she had never found her voice. You knew you didn't want to end up like her, a nightclub singer dressed in a gold slip-dress and muttering about beer at three in the afternoon.

"Here's the Voice Department, dear," Mother said. "Go ahead, pick your voice. And please hurry; I have a manicure appointment in twenty minutes. Let me know what you decide. I'll be over here looking at leopard-skin sling-back pumps."

You wanted a guitar, not a voice. You scoured the entire cosmetic, accessories, and sock departments without any luck. No guitars, no instruments, just voices. Rather than leave empty-handed you had to pick one. There they sat, your three voice choices: No Nonsense Fairy, Passive Aggressive Barbie, and Cussing Angel. The three of them squatted together on a white plastic shelf, too high for you to see, but low enough to hear every word, and close enough to smell mingled scents of Marlboro, lily of the valley, and flop sweat.

"Oooh!" said Passive Aggressive Barbie. "You don't have to take me. I'm probably not the best choice for an average child."

"What the fuck," said Cussing Angel. "Don't take her unless you really want to sound like a fluff-headed Barbie Doll. I'm your best fucking bet."

"Listen," said No Nonsense Fairy, hopping down from her perch. She wore an oversized green caftan with yogurt stains and a raveled hem. "Listen, you'll be fine if you take me. Listen, just keep your cool and remember to breathe. Listen, I know what I'm talking about."

"Why do you always start every sentence with 'listen'?" you asked No Nonsense Fairy.

"Listen," she said. "It's what happens when you grow up in a houseful of chattering nymphs—you learn to command attention any way you can."

"What the fuck," said Cussing Angel. "You should try living in the fucking choir loft with ten sopranos singing the Hallelujah Chorus on a loop. And this fucking halo gives me a migraine."

"Oooh!" said Passive Aggressive Barbie. "I had such an easy childhood. I guess I just don't relate to the middle class. Ooh! 'The human heart, like a feather bed, needs often to be stirred, sometimes roughly, and given a variety of turns, else it grows hard and uncomfortable whereon to repose.'"

"What the fuck is that supposed to fucking mean?" said Cussing Angel. "Are you quoting Mary Baker Eddy again? Give me a fucking break. Pass the barf bag."

"*Please?* Ooh! Manners, manners," said Passive Aggressive Barbie.

"What the fuck. *Please*. And fuck you, Babs."

༄

"Explain it to me again," you said to Mother as she checked her profile in a full-length mirror. "Exactly why do I need a voice? What if I don't want to be a singer? Couldn't I just get a bicycle? Why can't I have a guitar?"

"Oh, my dear, when I was a child, I never had a guitar. I had sugar thoughts and a honey mind, but also fears that tasted of vinegar," said Mother. "Oh God, I sound like a salad dressing recipe. Back in the old days, we didn't get to choose a voice or an instrument. It was assigned to us. At least you have a choice. If I were you, I'd think about Passive Aggressive Barbie. She has the most darling accent. And really, it's not such a bad thing to have a few Mary Baker Eddy quotes at the ready."

But you chose No Nonsense Fairy, mainly because you liked what she said about listening and breathing. Unlike your mother, you're still breathing. Big, cleansing gulps of air that leave you feeling loopy and free, if not exactly loved. Now, fifteen years later, you're still stuck with No Nonsense Fairy, a voice forced on you by riddle and neglect. At least you have your guitar.

No Nonsense Fairy doesn't like to fuss. She refuses to wear panty hose or makeup or dye her hair, and she insists you follow her example. "Listen, forget the henna rinse. Forget the support hose. Forget the peep-toe pumps. Be yourself."

Sometimes when you're busy being yourself you want to pick her up by the sleeves of her green caftan and fling her flimsy butt, gossamer wings and all, back to Neverland. Like right now, as you consider eating this pint of vanilla ice cream.

"Listen," she says. "Don't waste calories on plain vanilla."

"I'm allowed to like vanilla," you say.

"Listen, sister, life can offer so much more."

You swat her away. No Nonsense Fairy buzzes around the kitchen and makes that high-pitched mosquito sound you hate. She still smells like perspiration, the bad kind.

There's one thing No Nonsense Fairy can't stand, and that's string. Balls of string, pieces of string, stringy hair, string cheese, unraveling sweaters. She can't tolerate string, and she doesn't think you should either.

"Listen, strings get tangled." As a fairy she has spent her entire life avoiding objects that might ensnare her. She got trapped in a harp once, right in the middle of a love song. She barely escaped.

"Listen," she says. "Keep moving. That way you won't get caught."

"Thanks," you say.

"Listen," she says, "Here's your birthday present. You're twenty-three!" She slides a silver tray onto the table. You don't even reach for the cloud it holds.

No Nonsense Fairy smiles. "Listen," she says. "I'm out of here. My work is finished."

"Listen," you say. "Wait."

But she flies away, because that's what fairies know how to do.

You don't fly anywhere. You pack your guitar and take the bus to open-mike night at the Corner Café. Listen, maybe someone will listen this evening when you play your Joni Mitchell medley. You'll make No Nonsense Fairy proud. And at least you'll get a free dinner.

Silver

It takes Oliver Rosen eight and a half minutes to cross the Queensboro Bridge from Long Island City to Manhattan's East Side. That's on a good day, when he's not hung over and doesn't stop to stare at the jagged skyline. He crosses this bridge six days a week on his way to the Neil Simon Theatre on Fifty-second Street, where he plays flute in the orchestra of a Broadway musical called *Meet the Piggies*.

Oliver likes to stop in the middle of the bridge and look down at the silvery East River. Today, he jangles the change in his pocket and lets his mind wander. He drops a dime over the side of the bridge and watches it fall. Silver. He remembers icicles and scratched bike fenders; the smoky-silver fur of his favorite cat, Annie; his Aunt Stella's stiff and puffy hair, shot through with streaks of pewter and pepper; the dented pale silver Plymouth station wagon his father drove for the last two decades of his life; the shiny stainless-steel refrigerator, now in his ex-wife's kitchen; his daughter's charm bracelet with sterling trinkets that dangle from her thickening wrist; the Manhattan horizon on a cloudy winter evening, when the city lights buff the tarnished edges of an ordinary sky and turn it into a king's heaven.

Ten years. Ten years of playing for those fucking pigs. Not that he has anything against pigs. But Oliver Rosen, boy wonder of the Rochester Youth Symphony Orchestra, graduate of the Juilliard School, and prize-winning student of the esteemed Hank Goldberg, had expected more from his career than a ten-year run playing soaring flute lines for a bunch of pigs. Now, approaching his fortieth birthday, he is known in music circles as Pig Guy. He is divorced, living a thousand miles from his daughter, and trapped in an orchestra pit playing for Broadway's most beloved musical, whose highlights include an emotional Strauss-inspired waltz titled "This Little Piggy," and an extravaganza—featuring sixteen pigs and twenty dancers—called "Pork Pie Hoe Down." For Oliver, playing the show means two hours and eleven minutes of nonstop mind-numbing chromatic runs and trills eight times a week. Audience members tell him the pigs perform amazing tricks while he is playing.

The pedestrian path of the bridge—flecked with bits of fool's silver—looks endless and open and free, as if Oliver could stroll right into the amalgam of Manhattan's gaping mouth. But when he stands still, as he does today, the birds and cars and clouds and people and barges and buses and trucks and things that go-go-go make him dizzy with their collective sense of purpose.

Against all odds, *Meet the Piggies* had opened a few months after 9/11, just as other Broadway shows were closing due to dismal ticket sales. The threat of additional disaster kept tourists home—if terrorists could destroy the Twin Towers, what would stop them from blowing up a theater or two? Some shows stayed open, but panicked Broadway producers feared the worst—empty theaters and lost revenue. The producers of *Meet the Piggies*, "a delightful musical romp with an unstoppable porcine hero," went on with the show, determined to protect their investment by encouraging theater lovers to take advantage of discounted tickets. Most of the orchestra members, happy to have jobs, stayed with the show, but the original flutist hired for the gig, convinced that terrorists were targeting the Great White Way, fled to Montana. The musical contractor, desperate to find a virtuoso flutist willing to accompany dancing pigs, called Oliver after getting a recommendation from Hank Goldberg.

"Oliver Rosen is your guy," said the professor. "He's an odd sort. Persnickety. He wears a fur vest and these weird green fingerless gloves. And that hair? White guy with an Afro? Please. Or maybe he's not white, don't know. Don't care. Good player. Kind of a misfit, but he plays the heck out of anything you put in front of him. He's a scanner. He can read fly shit. And I've heard he's still unemployed, which doesn't surprise me, given his personality. If you can get past the ick factor, you'll have a great player in your pit."

The contractor hired Oliver, grateful to find a last-minute replacement who could nail the difficult score. So what if he wore a fur vest?

"The lead pig in the show—her name is Peggy P—speaks through the sound of the flute," the contractor told Oliver. "Your flute will be the voice of the pig. It's a tough couple of hours for you, since Peggy P is always onstage, and, basically, she never shuts up."

Oliver never imagined that a musical about a pig family, especially one that premiered so soon after America's greatest tragedy, would rescue Broadway, and, in a way, rescue him. Like most freelance musicians in town he was out of work and had been scrambling for gigs that didn't exist. His wife, frustrated by her temp work in a dental clinic, threatened to take their daughter and leave for Florida—which she did anyway, a few years later—but at least *Meet the Piggies* had bought Oliver a few years with his family.

Today is Wednesday. Matinee day. Two shows. Four hours and twenty minutes of pig music. It's lonely in the pit—Oliver's only companion is the conductor, a stout guy named Brownie. The rest of the orchestra is on the eighth floor of the theater building, connected to what's happening onstage through a video feed. Oliver keeps one eye on the video, one eye on Brownie, and tries to stay awake and in the zone. He's not sure how much longer he can stand it. The odor of overripe bananas wafts through the pit every time Brownie raises his baton. But maybe it's not Brownie. Maybe it's the pigs.

༺ ༻

Oliver stops again and looks at the river. The water heaves downstream, but it's dull and rigid, reflecting nothing—neither mystery nor magic surges beneath its thick skin. Oliver wonders what would happen if he opened his backpack, assembled his flute, and catapulted it, spear-like, into the river. Maybe it would bounce or float, but more likely it would slice through the façade of the murky water and vanish. Another contribution to Manhattan's moat. No ripples left behind. Gone. Poof. Just like that. Easy. Covered up. Vanished.

He had tried to get other work. Up until five years ago he auditioned for every advertised symphony and opera orchestra job he could find. He was willing to leave New York City. Oliver had come close to landing the second flute position with the Cleveland Orchestra, but lost to a Korean flutist who kicked his ass in the final round of auditions. Two years ago he had a shot at a tour with the rock star Baby. It paid five grand a week plus expenses. In the end, Baby hired a Spanish flutist who doubled as a flamenco artist. At one point Oliver tried to put together a flute quartet, but the gigs he booked paid barely enough to cover his expenses. He couldn't afford to quit the Broadway gig; he couldn't afford to send in a sub. He gave up on finding another music job and stuck with the dancing pigs. His wife and daughter gave up and moved to Orlando, where nothing is silver and everything is pastel. Once a month Oliver sends them money. Once a week he calls. Once a minute he misses them.

While he was still married, he had a brief affair with a substitute trumpet player named Grace. That could have turned into something, but she took a job with the Army Field Band and left town. Maybe later this week he could call her. Track her down. Tell her he got a divorce.

Oliver is the only original member of the orchestra and cast still performing with *Meet the Piggies*. Other musicians shift to other shows when they get bored, but Oliver, whose saxophone and clarinet skills are abysmal, stays, because no other Broadway show needs a solo flutist. He has seen chorus girls replaced by younger and leaner Broadway hopefuls. He has watched stagehands leave for better-paying jobs. Even the pigs retire after two years. Maybe they go to Florida.

The orchestra pit is covered with a transparent net that keeps the animals from sliding off the raked stage and into Oliver's lap. It happened once, back in 2008. The pig squealed, the audience howled, Brownie grunted and continued waving his arms. Oliver Rosen didn't miss a note. He continued playing while a frazzled stagehand soothed the poor pig, attached a leash to her jewel-studded collar, and led her through the bowels of the theater and back to the wings. When she reappeared in the downstage spotlight, glistening and serene in her silver tutu, the audience cheered.

Oliver looks down at the East River one last time, adjusts his backpack, puts on his headset, and listens to the opening phrases of James Galway playing the Allegro Maestoso movement of the Mozart Flute Concerto in G. Oliver has heard this recording hundreds of times. He never tires of it. The music sounds like polished silver—brilliant and old.

Oliver Rosen makes it to the other side of the bridge and keeps walking. He'll arrive at the theater in fifteen minutes if he keeps up his pace.

One more time. He can play this show one more time.

Taps

Master Sergeant Grace Elizabeth Wilson balances her eleven-month-old daughter on one hip while she runs through a series of warm-up exercises on her bugle. Arpeggio up. Arpeggio down. Grace's lip feels good—supple and stretched and strong—and she's positive today's ceremony will proceed as planned, despite the early spring chill.

Violet squirms in Grace's arms. Arpeggio up. Arpeggio down. How many times has Grace played this exercise? Ten thousand, twenty thousand. Something like that. The sound of the horn doesn't bother the baby—she's used to it—but Violet is hungry and it's past breakfast time.

"Where's your grandma?" Grace has a red ring around her lips, one of the hazards of the bugle trade. She looks out the window just as an icicle drops from the garage roof and lands like a dagger in the snow-covered flowerbed. "She should have been here fifteen minutes ago."

Violet, her head buried in Grace's shoulder, responds with a kick and a muffled yell.

"Okay, okay. Applesauce it is." Grace places her horn in the velvet-lined case sitting on the kitchen counter, sets Violet in her high chair, and grabs a jar of applesauce mixed with smashed carrots. Just as she opens it, she hears her mother's car in the driveway. She turns to look, Violet snatches the spoon, and a glob of the golden orange goop plops onto Grace's blue pants.

"Shit," says Grace. The baby cries. And in walks Grandma.

"Why is it whenever I show up you're cursin' and the baby is bawlin'?"

"Timing."

"Sorry I'm so late, hon," Grace's mother says. "The traffic was terrible cuz of a big old motorcade on the way out of the city. Must be a funeral at Arlington. Tied everything up. Is that the ceremony you're playin'? Must be someone famous."

"Shit," says Grace again. She runs to the sink and scrubs at her pants with a dishcloth.

"Language, Grace!" Grandma, still wearing her coat, begins feeding Violet. Violet laughs.

"Can you see the stain?" says Grace.

"No, honey. It's just a little wet spot. You look beautiful in that uniform. Or handsome. Or something."

"I look official, Mother. Like I have a job to do."

"Yes, you do. Official. That's the word. I never get tired of seein' you in uniform. Makes me proud. Reminds me of your daddy, bless his heart."

"Even with the applesauce stain."

"Even with. Have you lost weight?"

"No."

"Well. Your uniform is very slimming. I still need to lose a few pounds. I've given up pie and started bowling."

"Ah. The anti-pie diet. That usually works." Grace considers pulling her horn out of the case. She wants to continue her warm-ups, but, just as she reaches for her bugle, another car pulls into the driveway. It's a light green sedan. A military driver, wearing a white hat and gloves, steps out of the car and waits. This is the hard part. The transition from mother to soldier. You're in the army now.

Grace looks in the mirror. Invisible makeup, invisible emotions. Polished brass insignia, shined shoes, everything sparkling and new and crisp. There. Her hair is perfect for once, not a strand out of place and tucked neatly under her hat. She pulls on cotton gloves and kisses her mother goodbye. She kisses Violet goodbye, too, carefully avoiding the applesauce jar. They wave and smile at each other. Grace squares her shoulders, picks up her horn case, and steps into the soggy morning.

"Good morning, Sergeant."

"Private Demarco."

Demarco holds the door of the car for Grace. Before she slips inside she turns and looks through the kitchen window and waves again to her daughter. But Violet ignores her, choosing instead to stare at the spoon that feeds her.

༄

"Where are we going, Demarco?" Grace asks. "Arlington?" She usually plays formal funeral services for military elites—VIPs who die of old age.

"Not today, Sergeant. Quite the opposite. We're headed outside of Baltimore, to Woodpark Cemetery. Dicey area—close to the projects. It's a mess there. Local government tore down some of the public housing—blew the buildings up, actually—and there's a heap of rubble right next door to where those poor people live. Looks like a war zone."

"The fallen soldier—did he come from the projects?"

"Yes. But the deceased is a woman. The mother of the deceased requested a female bugler. Operations is lucky you were available."

The day thaws around them. Slush splatters the streets, trees drip, and crisp layers of ice crunch under the wheels of the sedan as they cruise through Grace's manicured neighborhood and onto the Beltway.

Grace's stomach flips over. Playing "Taps" is part of her job, but this is the first time she'll perform it at a young woman's military funeral. Since she left New York City five years ago, Grace has been a ceremonial bugler for the United States Army. It's how she makes her living. World War II veterans are dying off, and young soldiers continue to be slaughtered in Afghanistan or die long, slow deaths in the trauma units of military hospitals. Grace stays busy, busier than she was in Manhattan, where she had to do part-time office work to afford her music career.

Grace's father had spent his entire career in the military, first in active duty in Vietnam, later as a chaplain at Fort Hood, Texas, where Grace spent most of her childhood. She started playing the trumpet at age nine and began a parallel study of the bugle a few years later. Grace loved the bugle—the way the tones resonated, the subtle bounce of a major triad, the many moods created by so few notes.

Grace's father died five and half years ago, at age sixty. His medical records claimed liver cancer killed him, but Grace thinks complications from exposure to dioxin—Agent Orange—might have been the unspoken culprit. A hobby trombonist, he encouraged her to pursue a music career. "Leave," he used to say. "Go to New York. Make a name for yourself. Get out of Texas." After a four-year stint in the classical music department of the University of North Texas, she did exactly that. Her father, already weak from liver disease, stood next to the car the day she moved from Denton, Texas, to Manhattan.

"Go, Grace, go!" he said through the open window.

It took a few years, but Grace eventually picked up some work subbing in Broadway pit orchestras. The contractors liked her confidence, she could sight-read anything, and she was usually available at the last minute. She was warming up to play a silly musical called *Meet the Piggies* when she found out her father had died. Not quite sure what else to do, she played the show and tried not to cry. At intermission she called the contractor and asked him to find another sub for the evening performance.

Grace stood next to her mother at the graveside in Texas and wept for the man who believed in her and her music. The color guard showed up, the flag was folded, and then, much to Grace's shock, a real soldier with a fake bugle raised the horn to his lips and pretended to play "Taps." The sound came from the bugle, but the bugle was a toy, a boom box in the shape of a real instrument. The mournful sound of "Taps" fooled just about everyone attending the burial, but it didn't fool Grace. It broke her heart. Her father deserved better. The next day, when she inquired about the mime with the bugle, Grace found out the practice was commonplace—the United States Army didn't have enough buglers to cover all the military funerals.

Grace left Texas, returned to Manhattan, drank too much and ate too little, slept with a handful of married men, started a genuine affair with one of them, and then auditioned for the United States Army Field Band. When they offered her the job, it seemed like a good fit. Why not? Health insurance, a steady music gig, the chance to perform with great musicians. She could play, she could march, she could handle boot camp and a rifle, if necessary. And, with her ceremonial bugle skills, she could play at funerals, sparing other families the agony of listening to a fucking toy horn.

"Taps." Four notes. A major melody comprised of overtones. The saddest song in a long history of sad songs. Played graveside to honor those who have served. Performing "Taps" takes control and caution and confidence and compassion. Balance is key. Too much compassion, and the player loses control. Too much control, and she loses her sense of purpose. Too much confidence, and she'll cuff the high note or curl the edges of the middle tones. Too much caution and she'll run away from the grave, ashamed and weeping because she doesn't want to be part of a system that sends young men and women to shoot guns and drive tanks and face fiery deaths on frozen hills when they should be home reading books and planning careers and listening to music and taking care of small children in high chairs.

Stop. Now. She cannot think of these things. She must focus on the task ahead. Grace pulls her mouthpiece from her case and blows through it, keeping her bottom lip warm and nimble. She's happy she has remembered to take her beta blocker this morning. She cannot perform "Taps" without it. Her knees shake, her hands sweat, and she risks fainting. Fainting soldiers are not looked upon kindly by the ceremonial division of the U.S. Army.

"This might be hard today, Demarco."

"I'm sure it's never easy, Sergeant."

"Did you read the report?"

"Yes. Read it early this morning. The soldier was twenty-two. Military nurse. Mother of a toddler."

Focus. Now. Grace continues to push air through the mouthpiece as the March wind blows pieces of white plastic over the Beltway exit ramp.

"Nothing much left of her, from what I read in the report. IED hit her vehicle. God, look at this neighborhood, Sergeant. Terrible."

The car passes an Army recruitment sign. Be all that you can be. It looks like an invitation to glory.

After boot camp, Grace moved to Washington to begin her military music career. For several years she continued to see her married friend back in Manhattan. She cut things off with him when she discovered she was pregnant, or maybe he cut things off with her. Doesn't much matter. Grace's mother left Texas and rented an apartment nearby. She shows up almost every day to help with Violet. Grace's double life as a musician and mother feels purposeful. Really, she should count her blessings.

Anxiety curdles in her throat. The sedan rounds the corner and pulls through the gate. The slushy patch of gray-green cemetery plopped in the middle of the rubble-strewn subdivision seems glaring and artificial. This is not Arlington. It is a poor person's graveyard. Grace stares at the faint applesauce stain on her pants leg. She cannot watch a mother bury her daughter. She cannot watch a child stand at her mother's grave. She cannot. She just cannot. But she will, because this is her job and it pays for rent and food, and even though she's a musician she's also a single mother and a soldier.

Like always, a compassionate soldier with a stern face will drape a lonely American flag over the coffin. Family and friends will gather, shiver, and hold hands. The color guard will stand to one side, regal, respectful, reverent. A pastor will whisper words of solace that sound empty because hearts stripped of trust can never be again be full. Stoic and calm, the edges smoothed by Inderal, Grace will stand at attention when the color guard folds the flag into an impossibly small triangle and hands it to the soldier's mother.

To those attending, the ceremony will mean everything and nothing. Grace will raise her bugle and play her notes and stand up straight and hope her lip stays strong even if everything inside her collapses and caves and crashes in receding waves of sorrow for someone she doesn't know. Her bugle will shatter the silent spring with piercing streams of silver. Four notes will hold up the sky while they echo through the cemetery, layered like too many tears on a little girl's cheek.

The car stops next to a tented area by an open grave.

"What is her name?" Grace asks.

"Who, Sergeant?" says Demarco.

"The soldier," says Grace.

"Sorry, I've forgotten. It's in the report back on my desk. Chaplain will brief you as soon as he arrives."

"Thank you, Demarco. Do you mind if I get my horn out and play through some warm-ups in the car?"

"Not at all." Demarco steps outside the vehicle. "We have ten minutes, Sergeant." He closes the door.

The family of the dead soldier will hear real music this morning: real music played to honor a real woman who served her country. Grace places her bugle to her lips. Arpeggio up. Arpeggio down. If she does this enough times, she'll be ready.

Acknowledgements

Many thanks to the musicians who battle mega-rats, Voices of Doom, and bad catering so they can keep playing the music they love—music we need to hear.

A round of applause for Richard Johnston, my editor. RJ, if I ever write a Bad Ass Lois spin-off, you'll get the call.

A salute of gratitude goes to Jesse Kornbluth, who jumped in at the last minute with words of encouragement and advice.

Special thanks to my MRT musical advisors—brilliant players who helped shape my stories with their technical knowledge: Benyamin Nuss, John Goldsby, Karolina Strassmayer, Becca Rowan, Adam Nussbaum, Michael Sorg, Greg Thymius, Bill Mays, Christa Grix, Marvin Stamm, Loren Schoenberg, Bob Rawsthorne, and Emilee Floor. If I've gotten anything wrong, the fault is entirely mine.

Heartfelt thanks to Liesl Whitaker for inspiring "Taps." I can't imagine any musical endeavor more emotionally or technically challenging than playing "Taps" for fallen soldiers. Liesl, your talent is matched only by your bravery.

Thanks to Curtis Rawsthorne for his help with "Song for Alice."

Tip of the hat to Tracie Frank Mayer for setting me straight on the ups and downs of first class air travel. Baby can thank Tracie for that swanky first class lounge.

I will be forever grateful to my German friend, Nina. She went to battle with a real Manhattan mega rat, then had the good sense to tell me about it. Nina, "Pink" is for you.

Thanks to photographer Helge Strauss for his stunning cover image of saxophonist Karolina Strassmayer, and to Andreas Biesenbach for the author photo.

Many thanks to Christine Funke at Spark Virtual Assistance, for her help with technical matters. Christine designs my monthly newsletter, manages my mailing list, and keeps me from tearing my hair out over digital challenges.

Thank you to the fine people at Steinway & Sons, in both Hamburg and New York, who support my artistic endeavors with enthusiasm and generosity.

A big shout-out to Frank Baxter's Piano World Forum. My "Let's Talk Weddings" thread has garnered over 4 million unique views in the last few years. A writer needs readers. Piano World gives musicians a chance to be heard.

Sincere thanks to the fine women of FAWCO (Federation of American Women's Clubs Overseas), for promoting my work and giving me the chance to raise money and awareness for their current Target project. Please visit www.fawco.org to learn more.

Many thanks to my friend and fellow-writer Sharon Kae Reamer for her technical assistance with the structure of my stories. It's the Year of Courage, Ms. Reamer. Thanks for the push.

To my dear friends Leslie Brockett Wohlfarth and Robin Spielberg—your friendship means the world to me. Someday I shall write a song for you. Perhaps I'll persuade Baby to sing it. More likely, it will end up in the hands of No Nonsense Fairy.

Acknowledgements

A warm embrace to Bob and Ann, my parents, who have listened to me ramble on about these stories for three years. I'll shut up now, Mom and Dad, and let you enjoy your senior years.

To John, Curtis, and Julia—I love you more than anything. *Thank you* doesn't even begin to cover it.

About the Author

Robin Meloy Goldsby is the author of *Piano Girl: A Memoir; Rhythm: A Novel;* and *Waltz of the Asparagus People: The Further Adventures of Piano Girl.* Goldsby's career as a musician has taken her from roadside dives to posh New York City venues and exclusive resorts, and on to the European castles, grand hotels, and concert stages where she now performs. Robin has seven solo piano recordings to her name—*Twilight; Somewhere in Time; Songs from the Castle; Waltz of the Asparagus People; Magnolia; December;* and *Piano del Sol*—and has appeared in the USA on National Public Radio's *All Things Considered* and *Piano Jazz with Marian McPartland.* Robin is a Steinway Artist.

Robin often serves as a cultural ambassador for European organizations dedicated to transatlantic relations. In July 2012, she performed for German Chancellor Angela Merkel and former Chancellor Helmut Schmidt at the Eric Warburg Awards, sponsored by Atlantik Brücke, e.V (Berlin). She has presented her reading/concert program for numerous U.S. Consulates in Europe; for Amerika Haus, e.V. NRW; for Steinway in New York, Berlin, Oslo, Düsseldorf, and Vienna; and for the Federation of American Women's Clubs Overseas (FAWCO) in Marrakesh, Vilnius, Rome, Stockholm, Paris, The Hague, Hamburg, and Dublin. Goldsby's one-woman performance includes stories from her books along with her solo piano compositions.

Ms. Goldsby is the author, composer, and producer of *Hobo and the Forest Fairies*, a musical for children recorded by the WDR (Westdeutscher Rundfunk) in Germany. As a lyricist Goldsby has penned songs for Till Brönner, Curtis Stigers, Jeff Cascaro, Jessica Gall, Robert Matt, and Peter Fessler. In 2010 her collaboration with singer/composer Joyce Moreno, *Slow Music*, received a Latin Grammy nomination for Best Brazilian Album.

Robin currently lives outside of Cologne, Germany, with her husband—jazz bassist John Goldsby. You can visit Robin Meloy Goldsby's web page at www.robingoldsby.com Sign up for her free monthly newsletter and you'll receive a new RMG essay every month.

Also by Robin Meloy Goldsby

∽

Books:
Piano Girl: A Memoir
Rhythm: A Novel
Waltz of the Asparagus People: The Further Adventures of Piano Girl

∽

Essays:
Notes and Words
www.robingoldsby.com

∽

Recordings:
Somewhere in Time
Twilight
Songs from the Castle
Hobo und die Waldfeen
Waltz of the Asparagus People
Magnolia
December
Piano del Sol

Bass Lion Publishing is a multimedia imprint dedicated to quality music, music literature, and music education. Bass Lion controls publishing and licensing for compositions, recordings, books, and lyrics written by John Goldsby and Robin Meloy Goldsby.

www.basslionpublishing.com
www.robingoldsby.com

Made in the
USA
Monee, IL

14024021R00079